TEN STORIES THAT WORRIED MY MOTHER

WINONA KENT

WINONA KENT / BLUE DEVIL BOOKS

Print ISBN: 978-1-7773294-9-5
eBook ISBN: 978-1-7773294-8-8

Cover by Brian Richmond

Please visit Winona's website at www.winonakent.com
Please visit Blue Devil Books at www.bluedevilbooks.com

CONTENTS

Foreword by A.J. Devlin   1

1. TOWER OF POWER   3

About Tower of Power...   21

2. DIETRICH'S ASH   23

About Dietrich's Ash...   31

3. TRUE CONFESSIONS   33

About True Confessions...   43

4. CREATURES FROM GREEK MYTHOLOGY   45

About Creatures from Greek Mythology...   53

5. THE MAN IN THE GREY ELDORADO   55

About The Man in the Grey Eldorado...   67

6. HERD MAINTENANCE   69

About Herd Maintenance...   75

7. PERHAPS AN ANGEL   77

About Perhaps an Angel..   101

8. EASY WHEN YOU KNOW HOW   103

About Easy When You Know How...   136

9. SALTY DOG BLUES   137

About Salty Dog Blues...   165

10.   BLUE DEVIL BLUES   167

About Blue Devil Blues...   189

About the Author   191

Also By Winona Kent   193

FOREWORD BY A.J. DEVLIN

When it comes to writing, Winona Kent knows how to *rock and roll*.

In person or in her work, she will likely strike you as intelligent, savvy, with a hint of caustic wit. Despite being a multi-award nominated author, trained screenwriter, a tireless and excellent provincial rep for Crime Writers of Canada, and creator of the critically-acclaimed Jason Davey musician / amateur sleuth mystery novel series—at times Winona almost flies under the radar as an unsung hero on the Canadian fiction scene. As a result, I can think of no better way to see her talent showcased than through the ten short stories included in this anthology.

I could tell you how much you will delight in the surprisingly hectic behind-the-scenes late night action at a Winnipeg radio station, the eye opening and eclectic glimpses into Catholic schools and unusual vocations channeled into her work from her own life experiences, or the escapist whimsy felt when reading about coming-of-age, time travel, and tarot cards.

I could even guarantee that you will bebop along tearing through the pages of a couple of good ol' fashioned blues riffs that introduce you proper to her guitarist gumshoe himself or how one can make a strong case that the pitch perfect suburban vibe captured in a Tom Hanks eighties classic film could have been inspired by her humorous tale about a small-town ash tree.

But instead, I'll simply suggest this—find a comfy chair, sit back, relax, and take some time to go on a fast-paced and fun jaunt into Winona Kent's imagination.

I did, and not only was it enjoyable, but I came out a little bit wiser and great deal entertained upon finishing this collection.

Do yourself a favour, turn the page, and *rock on!*

A.J. Devlin

1

TOWER OF POWER

Warning: This story was originally published in 1982, and, as such, contains certain attitudes and situations, especially involving women and girls, which readers might find offensive. Please remember, at the time, those perspectives were real and they were pervasive. They most certainly do not reflect my own attitudes—either then, or now.

———◦———

Weeeeee are—number one!

"Better believe it, Winnipeg, this is Mike Windsor and on the line I have Sandy Abrahamowicz from the North End. Sandy has just won...a brand new $50 bill. Whaddya say about *that*, Sandy?"

"Great," she shrugs, using her best bored-sounding voice. "That's really great."

"Great? It's *dy-no-mite*! What's you're all-time favorite radio station, Sandy?"

"Uh...Tower of Power. Hitline, See-Rock."

"Far out, Sandy. In a minute, The Safety Pins—but first, this..."

Clearasil. If I hear one more Clearasil ad I'll puke. I check over the stacks of news stories displayed on the table before me like solitaire cards, and glance up again to find Windsor cleaning his fingernails, his mouth working furiously.

"What's your name, sweetheart?"

"Donna," whispers the little telephone voice.

"Donna what?"

"Donna Smith..."

"Where you from, Donna?"

"St. Boniface..."

"Whatcha up to tonight?"

"Homework..."

What a dog. Another snuggy. Dump her, quick.

"What can I play for ya, Donna?"

"I dunno...Hey, can you send a dedication?"

"Make it fast."

"OK, um...this is for Roger and Danny...and Jane...and my best friend Cynthia and..."

Windsor cuts it short. "Whaddya wanna hear?"

"Elvis Costello."

"See what I can do."

No chance—tonight's hits were picked by the program director yesterday.

"Hey, what's your all-time favorite Winnipeg radio station?"

Obediently, programmed by dark nights dreaming of her faceless hero, Donna responds: "Tower of Power, Hitline. See-Rock."

"Far out, Donna."

Click.

"See-Rock! Mike Windsor with all your hits on the only instant request line in the city! Three-three-seven, two-six-seven-three. These are The Safety Pins!"

He doesn't get to be original anymore, not in CROK's version of the packaged radio product. Between the hits you read liners from a mimeographed sheet tacked to a board behind the mic. Every third tune: a hitline reminder. Every ten minutes: a weather and temp update. And, anytime in between, a station and jock ident. He points his finger at me and it's my cue to pick up the copy and head for the newsbooth.

Hourly report. So-called news. I clip the cans over my ears and run down the intro.

"It's seven-forty-five, minus fifteen degrees Celsius, that's five above Fahrenheit. I'm Joe Randall with See-Rock News."

I lead with the story about the man who hanged three of his kids then shot himself in the head when his wife split town. Blood and guts. Clips from the lady who found them. Brains all over the carpet. The lights on Windsor's phone board wink on and off with the mechanical music. What good is information when it pre-empts Hits?

"Coming down in ten," Windsor yawns. With a bored nod, he flips a switch; a red light blinks on outside the studio door; I am On the Air.

"It's seven-forty-five, minus fifteen degrees Celsius, that's five above Fahrenheit. I'm Joe Randall with See-Rock News. Harvey Winkler of Steinbach won't have to worry about seeing his unshaven face in the bathroom mirror tomorrow morning. Harvey blew his eyes out this afternoon in what RCMP are terming a triple murder-suicide..."

Sometime after the drunks have called up for their hockey scores and the senior citizens have demanded their wrestling results, a guy dials the hotline to inform me there's a fire at the Riverview.

"Do I win the weekly cash award?"

"Yeah yeah. I'll put your name down. We'll be in touch."

"It's a really big fire, man."

"Anybody hurt?"

"Oh yeah, lots of ambulances. It stinks like a crematorium. Honest to God. Do I win?"

Get lost. "We'll be in touch." I beep the intercom and Windsor takes his time answering.

"Can you see the Riverview Hotel from your window?"

Begrudgingly, he cranks his head toward Main Street.

"Yup."

"Well is there *smoke*?"

"Yup."

For fuck's sake. This guy is a moron. "*Ambulances*?" I prod.

"Nah...Hey man, gotta go. Gotta cue a spot."

It figures. Manitoba Theatre Workshop. Clearasil. Time. Temperature. Cliff Richard. Buzz buzz buzz.

"Whaddya want now?" he groans.

"I'm going to get tape on the fire. Do me a favor, man. Watch the hotline? Half an hour?"

I'm wasting my breath. The jocks never answer the hotline. Asking is merely a formality.

I've sent memos to the program director in an attempt to rectify the situation, but these have wrought nothing but memos in return—reminding me to provide both AM and FM jocks with continuous updates on sports and weather. Why can't I work for CBC?

I grab my parka and shoulder the newsroom's Sony. There's a sticker on the case that says GOD IS MY SOURCE. Some Mormon sold it to me for a dime. I'm a real hit with all the born-again Christians.

It's a minor fire and a major disappointment. Mattress burning on the bed, heavy smoke, $1,500 worth of damage. Not even the couple who signed for the room can get excited. Too pissed. No injuries, not even smoke inhalation. I cut a voicer, and trudge back to the station.

Trying to get into CROK after hours is like trying to buzz the PM's bedroom. Management considers it unwise to issue its employees with keys so I'm at the mercy of Windsor, who has the power to ring me in whenever he gets my signal. The signal is a button—one of four screws in the mailbox panel on the door—which I must push. And they call this contemporary radio.

"Come on, you shithead! I'm on the air in ten!"

I might as well be screaming at the post office.

"Windsor!"

I'm tempted to throw rocks, but with my luck they'll shoot straight through his window and I'll be stuck for the bill. There's going to be a memo in the PD's box about this...

"For fuck's sake, Windsor!"

"Why are you yelling?"

I whirl around. It's a snuggy. No, too young, a snugette. Fourteen years old and hot to trot. Tinkerbelle.

"I'm trying to get into the station."

"It's no good. You ring and ring but they never let you in. I tried when Wolfman Jack was in town."

"Yeah, but I work here, sweetheart. They're *supposed* to let me in."

"You work at See-Rock? Really? Are you a deejay?"

"Sorry to disappoint you. News."

"Oh." She doesn't even try to hide her disappointment. "Same thing, isn't it?"

"No," I say, glaring at her. Is she a seasoned groupie with nine different diseases, including the one resistant to penicillin? Or does she just want to play fan with Mike Windsor? Wrong jock, kiddo. Wait for Donny Brooks. He likes 'em on the shy side of sixteen."

"Shouldn't you be in bed before ten?" I ask sarcastically.

She shrugs, the scorn apparent on her young face. I punch the button one more time and Windsor's voice screeches out of the intercom hidden in the mailbox.

"*Whaddya want*?"

"Lemme in, you prick!"

The lock buzzes; I grab the door, but the little groupie ducks in front of me and stands in the foyer, grinning, daring me to kick her out again.

"You can't come up to the studios."

"Why not?"

"Station policy." Blanket statement to cover everything from toilet paper to termination of employment.

"Aw, come on. I wanna see Mike Windsor."

"He's busy."

I turn and head upstairs. I don't want her walking into the middle of Windsor's shift or screwing up the monitor tape when I'm not looking. But—pitter-patter, pitter-patter—she follows me, all the way up to the second floor. I pause at the door to the newsroom. "Look, go home. You can't stay here, OK?"

"No."

"All right, OK, what do you want? A T-shirt? A record."

"I want to see Mike Windsor," she answers, stubbornly.

"I told you, he's on the air."

"When does he get off?"

"Midnight."

"I'll wait."

"But you can't wait here." She's just standing there, imagining she looks appealing. Miss Clearasil. I haul her into the newsroom and shove a chair under her skinny ass. "Sit. Do not move."

"When do I get to meet him?"

"After the news." I slip the cassette out of the Sony and ram it into the master deck, cursing the clock as it rewinds. There. I dub off three twenty-second clips. Somewhere out there, Knowlton Nash may be listening.

"Who's that talking?"

"Me."

"Doesn't sound like you."

"That's my radio voice."

"Yeah? Say something in radio voice for me."

"I don't have time right now." I am not Rich Little. I am not a performing bear.

She sulks while I scan the Extel for updates, rip the sheet and whip off a ten-line story about an overseas bus crash with fifty-two dead. Think I can get myself fired for making a joke about empty seats...?

"He doesn't *look* busy."

Windsor, visible through the glass window separating the newsroom from the studio, is sorting carts.

"OK, OK." I hit the intercom.

"What?" he asks, aggravated.

"This lady wants to meet you. What's your name, darling?"

"Debbie."

"Debbie wants to meet you. Mike, Debbie. Debbie, Mike."

Windsor nods and smiles benevolently. Debbie is disappointed.

"I didn't think he looked like *that*," she says, eyeing the Led Zeppelin T-shirt and the plaid Fortrel pants, the beer belly and the 32-year-old balding head.

"That's his radio face," I reply cleverly. "If you touch anything, I'll make him kiss you." I collect my carts and copy and, in a gesture of kind-heartedness, switch on the monitor for her.

Inside the booth, Windsor cuts into my headsets.

"Who's the snatch?"

"I dunno. I thought she came in with you."

"Send her over—my wife's in Florida. Coming down in eight."

"It's nine-forty-five, minus eighteen degrees Celsius, that's zero Fahrenheit. I'm Joe Randall with See-Rock News. A Calgary couple narrowly escaped injury this evening when a fire ravaged their downtown hotel room..."

There is no such thing as good news at CROK. It's a CRTC commitment, an appendix to the licensing agreement, a pain in the ass as far as management is concerned. If they could get rid of me, they would. In fact, they are. It's subtle, but the corporation, with its head office in Toronto, specializes in subtlety. *How to Control Staff Through Intimidation*. The first lesson is called "Paranoia." They don't come right out and fire you—they make life so miserable that you quit. I've seen it happen twelve times and I know it's coming down on me.

I used to do mornings. Morning back-up on AM, then reporting. Somewhere along the way the corporate executives changed their minds about me, so I'm getting tuned out. They don't expect me to resign for a while—not until they can find a replacement, anyway. But that shouldn't be hard. It's easier to can a night newsman than a morning back-up. Station policy. Fuck you.

"...call us on our news hotline: three-three-seven, N-E-W-S. See-Rock time...nine fifty-one."

Windsor leaps into the spot and I line up the sports carts. Someone sounding exactly like Debbie is attributing her Saturday night date to the use of someone's baby shampoo.

"See-Rock sports! The Jets lost another one last night..."

I hate sports but I only have to do three minutes, and as long as I don't use too many words like "nipped" and "thumped" I sound halfway credible.

"It's minus eighteen degrees Celsius—that's zero Fahrenheit. I'm Joe Randall for See-Rock News."

And I really cook the call-letters for Windsor as he takes me into an oldie by ABBA. Back in the newsroom, Debbie has finally recognized me.

"You're Joe Randall!"

"Only when I'm working."

"I hear you all the time—only I thought you were...I dunno. *Older.* Older and taller."

"Thanks."

"Howcome you're not in the telephone directory?"

"Because that's not my real name. Out of my way." I head for the tape deck.

"So what is it, huh? Your real name?"

"Randy Serbach."

"Cute. What's Mike Windsor's real name?"

"Herschel Sanderson."

"You liar. It is not."

"Ask him. Will you get outta my way?"

She struts over to the monitor, fiddles with the knob, and the station jingle slices through the air at a hundred and twenty decibels: "*Tower of Power...Just for yoooooooooo—fourteen-twenty...Seeeeeeee-Rok (Rok) (Rok (Rok)...*"

There he goes: "Nine-fifty-five in wonderful Winnipeg! Minus eighteen and howling! That's cooold, baby, but Mike Windsor's gonna keep ya *warm*!" He walks the vocals into Blondie, and his glasses flash Debbie's way. What's the matter, Herschel? Too close to your daughter's age?

I figure in a couple of years she'll be a hard-line groupie and I'll see her in the summer, hanging around the station door in her halter top. She has nice tits even now.

"Can I have a See-Rock T-shirt?"

"We don't have any."

"You said you did."

"Windsor gives them away, not me."

"Ask him if I can have one."

"Ask him yourself," I answer irritably. Right now I don't really care if she does walk into the middle of his talk set.

"Really? I can go see him? Hey, thanks a lot!"

The phone rings. "See-Rock news."

"Serbach!"

It's Rogers, the news director. A fat old bastard with a bright future in Toronto.

"How's it going, Serbach?"

"Not bad." I say not bad no matter what the situation. If I say slack, he tells me to work harder. If I say I'm running around in circles, he figures I can't handle the job. Subtle intimidation.

"Your nine-forty-five was a little rocky. Slow down your delivery."

"Yeah, yeah."

"How are you on all-night news?"

"*Why*?"

"Wilson's got car trouble. He can't make it in from Selkirk."

"Send him a taxi, for Christ's sake."

"You know my budget."

"Have a heart, Rogers. I got a lady at home."

"Quit your whining and do the job. You'll get overtime."

"Yeah, you pay overtime but not cab fare. Fuck you."

Rogers laughs. "Good night, Serbach. Sweet dreams."

Click.

I pick up the phone again, and dial home.

"Hello?" she answers sleepily.

"Hiya."

"What's up?" she asks.

"I gotta work all night."

"Shit! Why?"

"The usual crap. Wilson can't make it in from Selkirk, so Rogers says I have to cover."

"Shit."

"Yeah, I know. I'm going to be dead. How're you?"

"Cramps are still bad," she says, "but I'll dose up on 292s or something. If I'm dead when you come home tomorrow, you'll know why."

"If you get lonely...or anything...call me, all right?"

"Sure," she laughs, then adds, a little sadly, "Have a good night. Miss you."

"Miss you too. Take care of yourself, OK?"

"Yeah."

I honestly didn't believe it at first. I didn't believe it was happening to me. She did. She saw it coming. She watches the station like a hawk. She keeps tabs on who comes and who goes. She asks questions. She's a very intelligent lady—the type of woman all the jocks say they wish they could get their hands on but don't because they're all too busy sizing up the chicks with the big tits and cute asses but only half a brain between them.

I grab the phone one more time. We all know the newsroom is bugged but I have to take the chance.

"Good evening. Republic of Drackmolia."

"Dudek!" Oh *God,* let me speak to an intelligent news director in an intelligent place where they let you keep your real name on the air.

"Serbach, you old prick! What's new at Stalag-17?"

"The usual Gestapo techniques. Sorry to bother you at home, man. How's it going?"

"Man, you wouldn't believe it."

I can see him, the news director a CK-60, 25 years old and sitting cross-legged in his apartment, rolling a joint. No paranoia there.

"So how are ya, Serbach? How's the station?"

"Number one in the fall book."

"Bullshit, man. Have you *seen* the ratings?"

"I saw a bulletin..."

"Shit, you guys might be number one in *something*—toads over seven months, maybe—but it sure as hell isn't where it counts. I hate to disillusion you, old buddy."

"That's OK. How far can you expect to get with a rock 'n' roll format aimed at under-18 anyway?"

"That's right. Snuggies don't buy the time. I give you guys two more years till you drop. Ask to see the fall book, man. I bet they won't show it to you."

"They won't show us anything. Station policy."

"Serbach, you are an idiot. Get out, man. Join the Republic of Drackmolia. Why the hell are you still hanging around a two-bit station like Crock?"

I laugh. Now comes the Big Pitch. "Well, man, anytime you have an opening..."

"You serious?"

"What do you think?"

"How much you making over there?"

"Twelve-fifty."

Dudek whistles. "You ask a high price, man."

"Yeah, but I'm overpaid for night news. That's a morning back-up salary. They're trying to find someone to replace me for eight a month. I've seen it happen plenty of times. I know what's coming down."

Dudek is silent at the other end. Then: "Lemme ask around, man. Lemme call you back."

"Take your time," I tell him. "I'm here all night."

It's ten-thirty and I catch Donny Brooks checking into the studio to prep his show. There's another made-up name for you: this one came directly out of the station manager's scrapbook. He likes to finger stars. Before our big guy discovered the real Donny Brooks on an old k-Tel record, the sham Donny Brooks was just plain old Bob Jones.

Bob Jones is now sorting through the coffins, his bright red hair a strange contrast to the yellow and green mood lights in the studio. He looks like a little kid, with freckles and buck teeth and a baseball cap on the back of his head.

Bob Jones starts up a conversation with Debbie, who is perched on a stool behind Windsor, and I can tell the little darling is in seventh heaven. They leave together; there's a leather couch in the jock lounge upstairs. I hope he screws her little brains out.

I dub off five more voicers from the Extel machine and scan the copy for an update on the bus crash. Surprise, surprise, I'm ahead of schedule. Only two more newscasts and then I hit Wilson's night run. Too bad my lady didn't come down. She has before. She's spent hours in the newsroom waiting for me, reading copy, reading *Billboard* and *Variety*, reading everything in sight. She even wrote a news story once, about this bread made out of sawdust. It took her four rewrites and three-quarters of an hour to get the format and the kicker. All that for a ten-line story that takes me two minutes.

"Windsor!" I holler. "What's it like outside?"

"Winter! Get the hell outta my show!"

He doesn't care if someone like Debbie interrupts his all-important prattle. Fuck him. I slam the newsbooth door and lead off my ten forty-five major with dead Indians.

At ten to midnight, Debbie wanders back into the studio with Bob Jones. She's wearing a Tower of Power T-shirt which is three sizes too big for her, and her pink blouse hangs sloppily out of her macrame purse. Windsor exits, and Donny Brooks takes over, heading into his top-of-the-hour ident.

"Good morning, Winnipeg! It's twelve-oh-one with Donny Brooks. More music all the time with the Tower of Power, See-Rock Radio!"

I have nothing to do until two, so I head for the studio. Brooks is bouncing around the room, cans half off his head, bopping in time to Burton Cummings.

"How's it going, Randall, my son?"

He's the only lousy jock around here who'll even consider using my real name when he talks to me.

"Can't complain."

And you don't complain to Brooks. He's a company man too, in spite of his friendly exterior. I'm on my own here. All by myself.

"Can't complain about that little snatch!" he says, with a jerk of his head back toward Debbie. "Hey, d'ja hear about Whitcomb?"

"Nope."

"Whitcomb doesn't work for us anymore. Man, he'll be lucky to work in radio again."

"What happened? Did he besmirch the corporate image in some foul manner?"

"Worse. Hang on." He leans into the mic. "All the hits, all the time! Call us on the instant request line and we'll make it happen! Remember, we do it for *you*. This is John Lennon..."

He hits the pot and rolls back on his heels, grinning.

"Seems yesterday afternoon a call came in for Whitcomb. He takes it and man, he gets off the phone and he's just about in tears. 'My old man's just died,' he says. 'That was my sister.' And he heads out of the station, right? Well, the PD hears and says, hey, take off all the time you need, come back when you're ready, that kinda thing...and just to be nice he sends a bloody great wreath round to Whitcomb's place. Well, this morning the PD gets this call. It's Whitcomb's mother. 'What kind of a lousy joke is this?' she wants to know. 'Isn't Mr. Whitcomb dead?' the PD asks. 'No, he's right here,' says Whitcomb's mother, and there's Whitcomb's old man, on the line, alive!"

"No!"

"Yeah, man, the guy wanted a week off to be with his knocked-up girlfriend. Can you believe it? What a gross-out, eh?"

"What a stunt."

"Yeah, pretty poor taste. Hang on a sec. I gotta take some calls. Hi schnooks, who're you?"

"My name's Frank."

"Oh, ha ha, sorry Frank. What can I do for you?"

"Wanna score some weed, man?"

Brooks rolls his eyes up to the acoustic tiles on the ceiling. It's a good thing he's only taping, and the mic's not on live. "Yeah man, sure. Why don't you drop down and we'll do a couple of joins together?"

"Are you kidding? It's *freezing* out there!"

"Sorry man, that's the way it goes." Click. "See-Rock Hitline."

"Hi, Donny."

"Hiya, gorgeous."

I leave him to his following, and wander out to the reception area. On a coffee table in front of a little alcove where all the station awards are displayed is a present from some Tech-Voc shop class. It's the most grotesque monstrosity I've ever seen. The base is made out of goopy yellow acrylic, and growing out of this pool of acid are four wooden letters, C-R-O-K, sanded smooth and varnished brown. The 20th Century Fox of the broadcasting industry. The Tower of Power. With my fingernail, I trace around the bottom, skating on the plastic like Toller Cranston doing eights on a yellow ice slick. The acrylic is soft: I leave my mark. And lightly, ever so lightly, I inscribe, "Fuck You" in between the C and the R.

I shuffled back to the newsroom and turn up the TV monitor for the all-night movies. In a while I'll update the weather, but right now I want to relish my moment.

———◦———

About 3 a.m. Debbie puts in another appearance.

"I want to go home," she sulks.

"You can't. Unless you take a taxi, you're stuck."

"I don't have any money."

"Tough."

"Shit," she grumbles, plunking herself down on my chair.

"What do your parents think of all your little escapades?"

"They don't care."

"Too bad," I shrug, and I mean it. "Well, look at it this way. It's been a valuable learning experience for you. You met a real-live newsman."

"Big deal."

Big deal? Who brought you the tragic death of John Lennon in five instalments? Who keeps you all amused with regular features on Andy Gibb and Blondie? Who sacrifices real news for two-minute interviews with some dope who wears studs through his tits? Who are you shrugging off as a big deal?

"Go ask Donny to call you a cab."

"Can't you drive me home?"

"No way, lady. Maybe around six."

She sulks some more, her elbows on my copy table, and the telephone jangles me out of caring for her any more than any other snuggy who hangs around the station.

"See-Rock news."

"Serbach—it's Dudek!"

"It's three-thirty! Are you crazy?"

"Wanna job?"

For a second, I'm stuck for words. "Seriously?"

"Serious. Morning FM just opened up. Start tomorrow."

"Music for the Middle of Your Mind," I muse. "You're kidding, of course."

"Eleven-fifty a month. Start tomorrow."

Tomorrow. For a hundred-dollar cut. "Did you blow someone away?" I ask suspiciously.

"Naw—Henderson goddam quit on me."

"I have to give two weeks' notice..."

"That's bullshit, Serbach. If CROK could do it, they'd can you tonight."

I'm stunned. "Start tomorrow?"

"Tomorrow morning. Go home and sleep. Think about it. Call me back."

"Yeah...yeah...I will. Thanks."

I drop the receiver. What do I do? Stay and hack the system and get the boot when they discover my replacement lurking in Moose Jaw somewhere? Or quit, for a hundred-dollar-a-month loss, and do the kind of news that only elevator operators and dental assistants will ever hear? What a choice.

"What's the matter?" Debbie asks.

"Nothing. I just got a job offer."

"Yeah? Who from?"

"CK-60. Their FM station."

She makes a face. "My dad listens to CK-60 in his car."

"Yeah, and my girlfriend's hairdresser listens to FM while he's wrapping perms. Get out of my way."

"You're always telling me to get out of your way!"

"You're always in it."

———◄○►———

Twenty to four. I'm on the air in five. In the booth, I clip the cans over my ears. On the other side of the window, Donny Brooks is in pantomime with his mic, talking with his hands. He uses his hands a lot, pointing to copy, shaking them at records.

"Still with us?" he shouts.

"You bet."

"Coming down in ten."

Nine, eight, seven, six, five, four, three, two. "It's three-forty-five, minus eighteen degrees Celsius, that's zero Fahrenheit. I'm Joe Randall with See-Rock News."

———◄○►———

The phone rings and rings and rings. "Hello?" he croaks.

"Good morning, Mr. Rogers. How are you?"

"Who the hell is this? It's four a.m.!"

"It's Randy Serbach, Mr. Rogers."

"Serbach, you're up shit creek for this one! You've had it!"

"I resign. Two weeks' notice, effective now. I quit."

"You'll hear from us, Serbach. You'll damn well hear about this!"

Click. Debbie giggles. I have the phone on the monitor, and the tape reels and whirls around on the master deck. I flip it off and wait. Five minutes. Ten minutes. We sit like a couple of kids, knees up, smiling, waiting. There it is!

I grab the receiver, and Debbie hits the tape switch.

"Serbach, you're fired!" It's the PD.

"You can't fire me, sir. I quit ten minutes ago."

"I want you out of there tonight. No two weeks' notice, buster. You're out on your arse."

"That's fine by me. By the way, Henderson from CK-60 FM's available. Unless you already hired him..."

The PD ignores me. "You'll never work in radio again, you hear?"

"I'm leaving right now, sir. I'm just on my way out the door. Good night, sir. Sweet dreams."

I dub off six copies of the tape, and leave one in Donny's bunk in the studio. I tuck the other five and the master copy under my arm, and salute.

"Leaving already?" he asks, raising one red eyebrow.

"I just quit."

"No kidding! Got anything lined up, man?"

"That would be telling."

"You sly bastard. If this control room wasn't bugged I'd tell you what I really think. Stay cool, eh?"

"Will do."

"Seeya later."

Debbie waves bye-bye and zips up her shorty jacket. Outside, the wind is starting to gust, and Portage Avenue is a tunnel of blowing snow. My Datsun's engine turns over slowly, choking and gasping for air. I scrape the windows and climb inside, shivering, waiting for the heater to kick in.

Debbie has the radio on. She's tuning in to Donny Brooks and his bedcheck show.

"OK, Winnipeg, I'm gonna beam my little light right into your little beds where you're all tucked up cozy and warm tonight. You got a dedication? Lay it on me, man, I'm waiting just for you."

I can tell he's in close to his mic. This is a long talk set, way outside format limits.

"This one's for Debbie."

"That's me!" she squeals.

My summer tires spin and skid and send me halfway across the boulevard; I head down Donald to the Pembina Highway and Debbie's place.

"Far out," she sighs, as I drop her outside one of those white boxes known as low-income housing. "Wait'll my girlfriends hear about this!"

"Yeah, just wait. Here. A present for you."

I hand her one of the tapes. She drops it into her pocket, waves, and skips into the block. I make sure she's inside all right, then head for home.

She has the radio on CROK. She's asleep, drugged, hunched up in the bed with a shawl thrown over her shoulders and a tepid hot-water bottle scrunched between her thighs. She stirs slightly as I slip into the bedroom and pick up the phone and dial.

"Yeah," I say quietly, so as not to disturb her. "Hiya, Dude. It's Serbach. You got me."

"Far out, man. Drop by the station tomorrow and we'll introduce you and show you the setup. By the way, Rogers hired Henderson two days ago."

"Nice."

"Yeah. See you later. 'Night."

My lady blinks in the dim light. "You're home too early," she says faintly.

"I quit. I have a new job."

"Oh...where?"

"CK-60. Morning FM. Start tomorrow."

"That's nice," she says dreamily, and she's back in slumberland. I know she cares. It makes a difference. In the morning, when we can both talk decently, she'll tell me how much she really thinks of CK-60 and how they've always carried more weight with her than CROK. She will start to listen to CK-60 whenever she can. But, for tonight, it's still the old standby.

Donny Brooks pops over the air. "It's cold cold cold," he says, his voice rising with each word. "Gotta get my own weather tonight because my newsman ain't here no more, ha ha. Minus eighteen the low tonight, tomorrow's high minus five, current temperature at Portage and main—you guessed it—eighteen big ones below the metric mark. You're tuned in to the Tower of Power, See-Rock. This one's for my good pal, Randy. We're with ya, buddy! Three Dog Night, 'The Show Must Go On'!"

The circus organ intro dances through the darkened bedroom, and I listen with my head couched in my lady's arm. When the last notes have died away, I flick the radio to FM, and twist the dial down, away from 1420.

My new station is playing the Johnny Mann Singers doing cover versions of everybody. The computer runs the station at night. And I'm no closer to CBC than before.

But Dudek's hinted at format changes. They're going after CROK's tail this spring. They're aiming for older listeners, graduates from the CROK shop. Everyone knows the snuggies don't generate money. It's just a matter of time until the Tower of Power comes down. Just a matter of time.

About Tower of Power...

"Tower of Power" was written in 1981 or 1982, when I was living in Saskatchewan. Prior to that, I'd been living in Winnipeg, where my husband was a newsman for a couple of different radio stations.

I submitted the story to *Flare* magazine's fiction competition (back when *Miss Chatelaine / Flare* still published short stories). To my surprise, it won first prize, and was published, with minimal editing, in their September 1982 edition.

It was the first short story I'd ever had published (though not the first I'd ever written). It predated my first novel by seven years.

Some editing was necessary. As the editor told me, apologetically, they were a magazine with an audience of young, single women, and as such, they really couldn't publish words like *fuck*—much as she appreciated their context and authenticity in the story.

Radio people I knew back then swore a lot, and I was aiming for realism in the dialogue. But the *fuck*'s had to go. They were replaced with other euphemisms, which I always thought weakened the narrative, because they really didn't ring true. So in this restored version, I've put them all back in where they originally appeared.

There are also some very dated and frankly offensive attitudes towards young women and girls in "Tower of Power", but please remember that I was writing about attitudes that existed in the late 1970s and early 1980s. Those attitudes were real, and they were pervasive.

When I first moved to Winnipeg with my then-boyfriend (who later became my husband), he was working the evening shift from 5pm to midnight six days a week. I was working in a travel agency that was open from 9am to 5pm five days a week. We were living together, but I used to laugh that we only saw each other on Sundays.

On Saturday nights, I used to go down to the radio station, on the bus, and hang out in the newsroom for the last hour or two of my husband's shift. Everything you read in this story is a result of the observations I made during those visits. Randy's situation regarding his job security is very real.

"Tower of Power" is set in an era when they still had all-night news at Canadian radio stations. And they played real records—not computerized playlists. The outside temperatures were still provided in Celsius and Fahrenheit, six years after the Great Changeover to metric in 1975.

Randy's anecdote about his lady writing a news story for him to read on the air is true. As is his middle-of-the-night conversation with Dudek, who offers him a job.

It all really did happen that way.

2

DIETRICH'S ASH

Hey there. Looking to buy that house, are ya? It's been empty a good while, all right...You come on over to my place and I'll tell you all about it.

Myrna—put the coffee on. This guy's interested in Hubick's place.

That house? Two years old. Brand new. Used to be a vacant lot. Summer, kids used it for football. Winter—well, that was the home of The Henry Baker Maple Leafs. Best midget hockey team in the city.

Guess someone figured it was time to make some money on the place, though...Before we knew it, they dug a hole, and then the two-by-fours went up...and pretty soon, there it was, that split-level job. Pink and white. Two-car garage. All ready for some new owners.

Now, you can't call Myrna and me snoops. But the wife...well, you know what they're like. They gotta know everything. So, she figures, the best way to get caught up on the local chit-chat's to throw a party. A Tupperware Party. Mrs. Prosofsky, from the house on the end, she was there. And Wilton's wife—he teaches at the university. And Mrs. Dietrich—married to the German. Across the road. Next door to the new pink and white place.

Well, once those ladies got through trying out the juice pitchers and sandwich keepers, they got down to some serious gossip. And it came out that the new guy was a farmer. Name of Hubick. Made his fortune in wheat and figured he'd retire to the city.

He kept pretty much to himself, though, after the moving truck pulled away. Wandered around the front yard a lot...like he was restless. Sodded down the lawn. Put some seeds in along the driveway. Bought a hundred feet of garden hose down at Canadian Tire and kept it coiled around a tractor wheel hanging off the porch. But he never really was..

.sociable. Hell—we didn't even know he was married 'til Myrna caught sight of his wife one day, yanking weeds outta the grass like her life depended on it.

So you couldn't really blame us for getting curious, could ya? We spent a long time trying to figure out just how we were gonna to get to know the guy, and then my kid, Byron, he accidentally shot his frisbee over the farmer's back fence, and that solved it.

Because he had to hike in after it. And whaddya think he found on the other side of that fence? I'll tell ya. A farm. An honest-to-God farm. That guy Hubick, he had that quarter acre so full of crops, he could've put Safeway's right out of business. Beans up one side, corn down the other...beets...sunflowers...barley on the sundeck...canola under the cl othesline...

I said to Myrna, "If we had that kinda land out back, we'd put in a swimming pool."

And Byron said, "He has one of those too. A dugout. Right next to the summer fallow."

"The guy's a nut," I said.

"He's a farmer," said Myrna, "and some farmers just can't seem to get the prairie out of their systems. No matter where they go or what they do, they're farmers for the rest of their lives."

Myrna went to the university last year and took a course in psychology. She understands people.

You sure couldn't say that about Mary Dietrich, though. Like I said, they live next door to the farmer. And Mary, she likes to sit in her garden. She comes from England. Talks a lot about privacy—priv-a-see, she says, not pry-va-see—and a man's home's his castle, and four o'clock's tea time. In the garden. With biscuits.

So it turned out Hannah Hubick, the farmer's wife, figured four o'clock was the best time to hang out over the back fence and have a gab with Mary Dietrich about the weather. And putting up pickled beets. And lubricating the cultivator.

And Mary Dietrich told Myrna she figured the neighbourhood was really going downhill after that. What with the Boat People next block over, and that drug-addict guitar player on our side.

How's your coffee? Myrna's baking some macaroons. I'll go see if they're done.

I was wondering when you were gonna get round to asking about that tree. It does look kinda funny, doesn't it, stuck there in the middle of Hubick's driveway like that.

It's an ash tree. We all got them. City came along in 1967 and planted one to a family. It was a Centennial project. Neighbourhood Beautification.

All down this street they were real careful to put those trees right in front of the houses they were intended to beautify. I can tell you're confused. How does it happen, you're asking yourself, that Dietrich's ash is right in the middle of Hubick's driveway?

Well, I'll tell ya. Hubick's driveway used to be a whole lot narrower. And Dietrich's front yard used to be a whole lot wider. Because Dietrich's property line used to end just the other side of that ash tree, that's why.

In fact, that property line used to look a whole lot different from the way it looks now. For one thing, Dietrich used to have a white picket fence and rose bushes to mark the boundary between his place and next door's. The fence was Mary Dietrich's idea, coming from England and all. Her husband was the one who planted the roses. All the way down the driveway, from his house to the sidewalk. Red, white and pink. Dietrich really loved those roses. He was always out there, making sure they didn't get aphids or powdery mildew.

That farmer, though, he didn't think much of that white picket fence.

One afternoon, Myrna took a look out the living room window, and she saw Hubick, pacing up and down, one end of the driveway to the other, scratching his head and muttering and giving that fence the evil eye.

And then in the night, when the moon was full, we heard things. Strange noises. Chopping wood.

And whaddya think we saw in the morning?

Dietrich's white picket fence in pieces. Not just in pieces, but in little pieces, all piled neatly, one on top of the other, on the other side of the rose bushes. So now, it looked like all the roses belonged to Hubick instead of Dietrich.

Well, Myrna got on the phone to Mary Dietrich right away.

"I can't think!" says the German's wife, in her Buckingham Palace voice. "I'm ashamed to show my face. This would never happen in England, where one's home is one's castle!"

Turns out there was some kinda glitch in the original survey line. And the German was sitting on too much land. So the farmer was only claiming back what was rightfully his. And, to make it worse, Hubick wasn't too keen on foreigners. He figured they caused wars. Figured they were behind the high interest rates and unemployment and falling wheat prices.

Well, that's when the Tupperware parties started up again. We got so many juice pitchers and sandwich keepers we had to give half of them away to the mother-in-law. In the end I guess it was all too much for Mary Dietrich. She went back inside her house and never came out again. Kept the curtains closed all day and all night. Wouldn't even answer the phone.

We didn't see a whole lot more of Hubick, either, 'til the summer was just about over and all the crops were in and the farmers were ploughing the stubble into their fields outside the city. That's when Hubick started staring down Dietrich's property line again.

Myrna's always got her nose stuck in those supermarket papers, and on one particular day she came across something she thought I oughta see.

"Look here," she said, and she held up the page. (I thought it was about the story called "Aliens Stole My Brain for Sex Experiments" but it was about the one underneath.) "Look here. I think Mr. Hubick has some kind of peculiar Mental Illness. I think Mr. Hubick has the opposite of agoraphobia."

"What's agoraphobia?" I said, because she had the advantage of that psychology course at the university, and I didn't.

"It's a fear of open spaces," Myrna said. "And I think he has the opposite of that. An extreme form of claustrophobia."

"Claustrophobia," I said, looking out our window at the farmer.

"Suburbaphobia," said Myrna. She learned a lot on that course.

A couple of days later, he was out there again, standing in the middle of his driveway, waving his arms around like he was directing traffic. You know who he was waving his arms at? Some survey guys, with tripods and maps. And whaddya think they found?

I'll tell ya. Turned out that farmer owned even more land than he thought. Six feet wide and twenty feet long, all the way down the line of rose bushes. One hundred and twenty square feet.

The German, he gets home from work and he has to look twice. Half his goddamn yard's pinned down with twelve-inch stakes and orange flags.

"What is going on here?" he says, standing there all hot and bothered, with his tie loose and his collar open.

"Well," says the farmer. "I reckon you got a hundred and twenty square feet of my land. And I'm just takin' it back."

"What is wrong with your own land?" says the German. "Is it not enough?"

The farmer, he just scratches his chin some, and then looks up at the sky. "Driveway's not big enough," he says. "Gotta have more room there. Driveway's not near big enough."

The German, he's gettin' all red in the face now. "How much room do you need for the pickup truck?" he says. "And why do you not park it in the road, like the rest of us? You are the only person here with a driveway!"

"Gotta have more room." That's all the farmer says, and he turns away. "Gotta have more room."

I'll tell you somethin' else. The next morning, Myrna, she looks out the window, and whaddya think she sees? Dietrich's roses, all cut into twigs. And Dietrich's front yard—everything on the driveway side of the orange stakes—cultivated into furrows.

"Goddamn, I wish that fella would do his dirty work in daylight," I says. "What's he got against the sun, anyhow?"

But Myrna, she's already on the phone to Mary Dietrich. Has to let it ring fifteen...sixteen times. "He didn't even ask!" wails the German's wife. "He didn't even ask. And now they're all dead. Our lovely English roses!"

"It's a shame about your priv-a-see," says Myrna. And then she tries to tell Mary, maybe if she sticks the twigs into water or something, they'll put down roots. But Dietrich's wife won't stop howling long enough to listen.

"This horrid, horrid country!" she wails. "That horrid, horrid man!"

She said the same thing to Hubick, too, the very next Sunday. Stuck her head out the front door and hollered at him. "You horrid, horrid man!"

Well, the farmer, he just rolled down the window of the pickup and made some kind of remark about Dietrich being foreign and responsible for World War Two and every gopher hole in Western Canada. And then he headed off to church with his missus. And when they came back, he got changed into his striped overalls and his John Deere tractor cap and he stood there in his driveway, glaring at those survey stakes.

And then he went for his axe.

It was that tree. Remember that ash tree the city planted? Well, damned if that tree wasn't sitting bang in the middle of Hubick's one hundred and twenty square foot annexation. City never figured on the survey line being wrong.

Well, that farmer, he didn't care all that much about neighbourhood beautification. The way he saw it, that tree was in his way. He let a good piece of spit fly onto the blade of that axe. And then he hiked it up, over his shoulder, ready to swing.

Just about that time, Dietrich was taking a look out his front door. And you can guess what he was thinking when he caught sight of Hubick, getting ready to take a whack at his favourite Centennial project.

"You!" he says, running out of his house. "You! *Halt!* How dare you chop down this tree!"

The farmer, now, he figures maybe he'll try to fool the German a little. "It's sick," he says. "It's sick, and I'm doing you a favour."

"Sick?" says the German. "*Sick?* What is sick with?"

"Dutch Elm," says the farmer.

"Dutch Elm?" Dietrich hollers. "*Dutch ELM?* This is ein *ASH* tree!"

"Dutch Ash," says the farmer. Didn't even blink.

"*Schmuckfatzen!*" Dietrich bellows. "I make Dutch Ash out of you!"

"Can't see the road," says the farmer, lookin' up through the branches. "Can't see the prairie. Can't see the sky."

"Ah!" says the German, glaring. "Then why do you not also chop down McWhirter's house? Is in the way also, no?"

And he points right at us. Jesus. Myrna, she whips the curtains shut real fast, and we go flat against the wall. We sure wouldn't wanna be known as snoops.

"Anyway," says the German, with a jerk of his head. "Is not your tree to chop down. Is not even my tree. Is City tree. And is forbidden to destroy City property. So there."

The farmer, now, he has to think about that. He never figured that tree belonged to anyone but Dietrich. And he's thinking so hard, he forgets all about his axe. And the German, he sees all those little brain cells distracted, and he knocks that axe right out of the farmer's hand.

Well, that's when the neighbours all came out to watch. Wilton, he was writing it all down in his journal. And Prosofsky's kids brought out the Cheezies and Coke. My own kid, he popped some film into his camera and started clicking, just as Hubick dumps the German in the driveway and heads off down the street, swinging that axe.

SWACK! SWACK! SWACK! He's taking swipes at just about everything painted green. Boat Peoples' Datsun. Wilton's garden gnome...SWACK! Pretty soon, the cops are rolling up, and he starts taking swipes at them too. SWACK! And he heads off round the corner and down the lane, and through Prosofsky's yard and back out onto the street again, the cops on foot, chasing after him.

"This man!" Dietrich's hollering. "This man is a menace to democracy! This man must be arrested! This man is *submersive*!"

Well, they finally collared the guy. Got him when he tried to climb up the ash tree. Grabbed him by the belt and dragged him down and snapped the cuffs on. Hauled him over to the squad car and dumped him in the back seat.

"You," says the German, glaring at him. "You. I show you Dutch Ash..."

The kid, he got a good shot of the farmer with his camera. Here it is. See the look in his eyes? Like that tree was dangerous. Like the whole goddamn neighbourhood was out to get him.

Myrna stuck around till the cruisers drove away and everyone else went home. They were real disappointed. I mean, we figured we'd see an axe murder for sure.

"You think he'll go to jail?" she says.

"No way," I say. "The guy's a fruitcake. Coupla months with a shrink, he'll be on the loose again."

"I wonder," says Myrna, "if he'll ever come back to this neighbour-hood."

I shook my head. "I bet he goes back to his farm. Can't live in the city. You said it, Myrna. Suburbaphobia."

Well, that's the house, right there. That pink and white job. Still up for sale. Been empty since he got hauled away. The driveway needs a little repair...gotta work around that tree. But what the hell, you can't beat the price, eh?

ABOUT DIETRICH'S ASH...

An earlier version of "Dietrich's Ash" was an Okanagan Short Fiction Award winner and was published in *Canadian Author & Bookman* in Winter 1985. It was also anthologized in *Pure Fiction* (Fitzhenry & Whiteside) (1986) and broadcast on the CBC Radio program, *Ambience*.

The story was inspired by an unfortunate situation that arose from a disputed property line between our house and our neighbour's house when I was growing up in Regina.

The farmer, the couple who lived across the road, and Mr. and Mrs. Dietrich are no longer with us.

The ash tree...

(Checks Google Street View...)

...is still there.

3

TRUE CONFESSIONS

I'd arrived at my assigned job promptly at nine—J. Child and Sons, Builders—its offices occupying what had once been a detached brick house, the remnants of its ample garden paved over and now used for parking, storage and a collection of sheds, the house itself displaying numerous signs of alterations and renovations.

I knew the drill—I was a veteran of two previous jobs. Introduce yourself to the person named on the Assignment Sheet, let them show you around and explain what needed to be done, settle in and get to work.

I'd opened the front door—it wasn't locked—and obeyed the sign directing me upstairs.

Nobody.

I wandered down the hallway and peeked in all the offices.

Deserted.

My Assignment Sheet said I was going to be working in "Reception" as a clerk/typist. "Reception" was located behind a door in what had once been a front bedroom. I opened the door, and surveyed my domain.

Desk with a typewriter—a clunky manual Underwood—and a phone—black plastic with a row of red and white buttons along the bottom that terrified me. I was no good with buttons that put callers on hold while you transferred them to another extension. Regulation swivel chair. One bank of grey filing cabinets. A coat rack in the corner and a large, flat window masked with dusty venetian blinds. The view from the window was of the yard below, and the brick houses across the road.

At the agency, Vanessa had informed me—employing that special whisper she reserved for those with not a lot of experience—that J. Child and Sons was one of the largest, most important building firms in Kilburn. Their regular secretary was on a two-month break, and the last temp Vanessa had sent over had quit with no notice. I would do well to take the assignment. And I would almost certainly profit from it.

"And," she'd added, almost confidentially, "I'm told they have a little garden on the roof! That'll be nice on your tea break!"

I almost certainly *would* have profited from it...if there'd been anyone around to actually tell me what they wanted me to do.

I took off my coat, hung it up on the stand in the corner, and sat down behind the desk. I had a terrible thought. Was I even in the right place?

J. Child and Sons, Brondesbury Road, NW6.

Yes, absolutely correct. There was stationery in the top drawer confirming it.

Well.

<hr />

It was now half-past nine and I'd decided to reorganize the contents of the desk. Items of a secretarial nature now lay in neat little heaps before me: red and blue striped stick pens, yellow pencils tipped with nubby pink erasers, vials of sticky white correcting fluid. A jar of hand cream, its label greasy from repeated dips. Letterhead, crinkled carbon paper, self-sealing envelopes embossed with the firm's return address. An Oxford dictionary, its spine uncreased.

At the bottom of the desk, in a drawer that had protested as I'd tugged it open, I'd discovered a radio. And underneath the radio, concealed like a guilty passion—a magazine. *True Confessions*. Heart-rending sorrows and intimate agonies. It was the kind of publication I would smugly avoid while buying my copy of *The New Yorker*, then secretly glance at two days later at the grocery checkout.

It wasn't a British publication, though. Whoever usually occupied this desk was getting it sent over from America: there was a little subscription label at the bottom of the front cover.

I removed the radio and kicked the drawer shut. The tuner was broken, the volume knob cracked in half. Nevertheless, I switched it on and the relaxing voice of Brian DuValle filled the room, placid as a midmorning cup of weak tea.

"In a moment, girls, an absolutely marvellous new recipe for Fruit Flan...and, coming up—DuValle's Daily Household Hint. But first, back by popular demand—Val Doonican."

I hummed along. As a particularly syrupy crescendo peaked, the door to Reception flew open and a short woman in a mauve coverall marched in, armed with a long-handled purple mop. Her face was the colour of a dredged powder puff. A crumpled cigarette smouldered between her Flaming Passion lips.

"You from the agency?"

"I am," I confirmed.

"You're in too early. We wasn't expecting you 'til later."

"I was told to be here at nine."

"Well," the charlady sniffed, "old Mr. Child don't stop by 'til after ten. None of 'em does."

She plodded over to the window, and gave the venetian blinds a flick with a rag she pulled out of her apron pocket. "American, are you?"

"Canadian, actually."

"Sandra," she said, sniffing again, "that's our regular girl, Sandra—she's seeing an American bloke. I hope you're not one of them illegal immigrants." She was glaring at me, puffing furiously on her cigarette.

"No," I said. "No—I'm only visiting. I'm going home—to Canada—in September."

"Mind you do then," she warned. "There's too many bloody foreigners about these days. And half of 'em's on the dole. Don't even want to work. Lazy buggers."

She peered out of the window, holding the blinds back with the handle of her mop.

"And don't you go spilling nail varnish remover all over that desk the way the last girl did. Talk about never wanting to work!"

Satisfied the road and the front yard were still there, she came back to confront me.

"Let's have your name, then."

"It's Carol," I said. "And what's yours?"

"Mrs. Thatcher. And don't you go calling me Maggie or The Iron Maiden, or I'll clobber yer. It's Hilda. Hilda Thatcher." She shuffled back to the door. "I'm going to put the tea on. You mind what I said about nail varnish remover. Bloody nerve."

I was disappointed. I had hoped for a longer visit. There was so much more to know about Sandra, who favoured Brian DuValle and kept simmering and dangerous romances locked in her bottom drawer. And the last girl from the agency. Did she lacquer her nails with Dusky Rose, or Raspberry Creme? And Hilda Thatcher, the Mop Maiden. Was it she who spearheaded the British advance on the Falkland Islands?

And when was someone going to show up to tell me what I was expected to do in Sandra's absence?

<hr />

"Quarter to ten, ladies—that's fifteen minutes before the hour of ten o'clock, on the Brian DuValle Morning Frolic..."

I wandered out to the hallway, where there were some stairs going up to what I hoped was the roof-top garden.

Mrs. Thatcher was busily mopping her way toward the offices at the back of the house.

"Hello?" I called.

Mrs. Thatcher stopped and glared around at me, veiled in cigarette smoke.

"Do these stairs go up to your roof garden?" I asked.

"Aye," she said suspiciously.

"Am I allowed to go up there?"

"You can if you go by yourself. I'm not obliged to accompany you. Not with these legs. Not with my lumbago." She waddled towards me, pushing the mop before her. "Our Sandra's always trying to get me up there. 'Come on, Mrs. Thatcher,' she says, 'come on, Mrs. Thatcher—come up and help me water my tomatoes.'"

I raised an eyebrow. "Tomatoes?"

"Aye," said Mrs. Thatcher. "Tomatoes. In crocks. And geraniums. And I don't know what else. I reckon she's growing cannabis."

She poked me in the shoulder.

"I reckon that hoodlum boyfriend of hers put her up to it. Don't you tell me he's a good, honest lad. He's American. Drug addicts, the lot of you."

"I'm Canadian," I said.

"Six of one, half-dozen of the other. You mind yourself. There's some very funny business afoot up there, let me tell you."

───────────◇───────────

The garden was a lush little island in a sea of sooty rooftops, complete with a green park bench, several striped deck chairs, an imitation marble patio table, and a patriotic red, white and blue beach umbrella. The tomatoes and geraniums were flourishing, the ripe dazzling reds a brilliant contrast with the grey brick and cinder-gravel underfoot.

There was no cannabis.

There was, however, a magnificent view of the city. In front of me spread a vista of attics and slate tiles, crumbling chimneys and speckled pigeon perches. A church steeple gleamed silver in the brown morning haze. Away in the distance, across the railway line and over the rooftops, was London. Real London, not just an appendage in the *A to Z Street Atlas*. Real London, where cars and buses and taxis rushed around the streets, Underground trains rattled beneath them, and the pace of commerce was frantic.

Not like sleepy little Brondesbury Road, NW6.

I wondered whether Vanessa would ever risk sending me into the city. After all, she had the reputation of the agency to consider. I was not what anyone could seriously consider a seasoned temp. I wasn't even a proper secretary. I was Almost-a-B.A.-in-English, a student on holiday in London for the summer, with one month's practical experience in the bag. I'd made up my references, gambling that nobody was going to bother to call Canada to check them. I could definitely type, but my skills didn't extend as far as shorthand. I was willing to tackle Dicta. I had rudimentary knowledge of filing. And I was ok on phones, as long as I didn't have to Hold and Transfer.

───────────◇───────────

"It's now ten past eleven, girls—that's ten minutes past the hour of eleven o'clock—and time for a nice pot of tea. Come on, ladies, put your feet up, pour yourself that cuppa, and have a listen. This one's especially for Joan, of Bonneville Gardens in Clapham, and for Georgette, of Angus Road, Brixton. Just for you—Des O'Connor."

The voice of the terraced houses (identical except for their brightly painted front doors and matching window frames), soothing and complacent. I yawned. Thankfully, there had been no telephone calls since I'd vacated the roof. No one bearing the surname Child had appeared to build upon my solid foundation. Much more than this, I thought, and I would have to revert to the *True Confessions* hidden away in the bottom drawer of the desk.

I touched the handle, then changed my mind. No. Anything but that: an affront to my university education, an insult to a fan of even the most farfetched fiction. Mindless pulp. *Never!*

I was saved by Mrs. Thatcher, barging in with the tea. "You got a boyfriend? Sandra's young man rings her up once an hour, punctual, just to inquire after her health." She placed the cup and saucer on the desktop. "Where's your fella?"

"In British Columbia," I replied. "In a lumber camp. Studying forestry."

"Not much of a future there," Mrs. Thatcher sniffed. "Married to a bloke who chops down trees."

"I'm not going to marry him," I said. "And he doesn't chop them down, he studies them."

"You're all alike, you liberation girls. You need to get wed and stay at home and have children. Then we'll see what happens to this country's unemployment rates."

"Mrs. Thatcher," I said, "I am not ready for marriage. And hungry babies howling at me in the middle of the night? No thanks. And I seriously doubt removing women from temporary secretary jobs will have much of an impact on the ranks of unemployed men."

"Suit yourself," Mrs. Thatcher sniffed.

She rubbed the corner of my desk with her rag, where the last girl's nail varnish remover had puckered the lacquered finish.

"That old Mr. Child's a miser," she said, confidentially. "I've told my Fred if I don't get a rise in my wages next month, I'm giving notice. Didn't even want a temp to fill in for our Sandra, he didn't. It was his son-in-law, Mr. Edson, that persuaded him in the end. Said we couldn't get by without a proper girl, what with answering the telephone and seeing to visitors and that."

"Yes," I said, "and it's so busy."

"And I'll tell you something else about our Sandra. She's not really on holidays. It's woman's troubles. Down *there*."

She spewed out a cloud of blue smoke. And I'm sure she was about to provide further tantalizing details about Sandra's medical condition, but she was interrupted by someone opening the Reception door. That someone was a man wearing battered jeans, an open-necked shirt, and a rather worn-looking pullover. Mrs. Thatcher shot him a downtrodden-oppressed-masses glare, then shuffled out.

"Are you the girl from the agency?" he asked.

"Yes," I replied. "Carol."

"Jack Edson. Old man in?"

"Not yet," I said. "Nobody here but me and *The News of the World*."

Mr. Edson laughed. "We only keep her on because her husband's chronically unemployable." He checked his watch. "Tell you what, though, if the old man staggers in and hears that radio going, he'll have your head. Instant dismissal."

"Oh. Sorry." I silenced Brian DuValle. Back to the bottom drawer with you.

"Just a friendly warning. Sandra takes it up to the roof when she has her lunch. Old man can't hear it up there. Sandra's our regular girl."

"Mrs. Thatcher can't say enough about her."

"I can imagine. Lucky girl's gone on an extended tour of Scandinavia with her boyfriend—in spite of Hilda's theories concerning her state of health." He checked his watch again. "I'll see you later. Tea up?"

He didn't wait for a reply. I stuck my chin on my fist and wondered whether a strike somewhere had resulted in a complete work stoppage and that was why no one was around. Electricians? Plumbers? The corner shops were just getting over another sugar shortage, and there was still a countrywide lack of toilet paper. Was Kilburn's most important building firm about to topple from lack of trade?

If only my learned professors in Canada could see me now, I thought. Scholarship student. Innovative. And unable to come up with a single way to keep herself occupied in the absence of assigned work.

She, who had once written an essay comparing Milton's *Paradise Lost* to a charter flight to Hawaii. She, who, in another treatise, had discussed the elements that Restoration Comedy had in common with Sid James's *Carry On* films. She, who had boldly dared to hand in a paper declaring that E.E. Cummings' *The Enormous Room* was not, in fact, a novel at all, but really just An Enormous Poem.

The jangle of the telephone jolted me out of academia.

I picked up the receiver.

Nothing.

I put it down again.

The phone kept ringing.

I stared in utter confusion at the panel of red and white buttons. One of them was flickering uncertainly. I tried not to panic. I pushed in the button and picked up the receiver again.

There was a click, followed by—nothing.

"Hello?" I whispered.

Silence.

I punched the next button in the row and got a purring dial-tone.

I went back to the first button, the one that had been flickering, and pushed it in.

Dial-tone.

Congratulations, Carol, I thought. You have successfully disconnected your first caller.

I waited, willing them to ring back. What if it was Vanessa, checking up on me?

Next time I would lift the receiver first, and *then* start pushing buttons.

The line flashed once more. The familiar double-British-ring echoed around the room.

I picked up the receiver. I pushed in the button.

"Good morning," I said. "J. Child and Sons."

"Jack Edson, please."

It wasn't Vanessa. But it was a woman.

"Hang on," I said.

There was no way I was going to cut her off again. I placed the receiver on the desk and dashed off down the hallway.

"There's someone on the phone for you," I said, poking my head through one of the open doorways, directing my comment at the man in the worn-out pullover.

"Ah," he said, a trifle surprised. "Very good. You might have used the intercom."

Intercom? I could barely get the phone connected, and he expected me to master an *intercom*?

"Who is it?" he asked.

"I don't know. A woman."

Memos will fly at the agency about this, I thought. "Carol Johnston is fit only to study Chaucer and Vonnegut. She is a disgrace to the Honourable Society of Temp Secs. Send her back to university immediately."

"Can you transfer her?"

"I'm not quite sure how your phone system works, actually."

Mr. Edson got to his feet and followed me, patiently, back to Reception.

I slumped into my chair behind the desk as Mr. Edson picked up the receiver. Really, I thought, I'd have been better off attending summer lectures at Oxford or Cambridge. Concocting more of those imaginative essays. Secretarial work was all very fine if you primed your life with Brian DuValle, weak tea and *True Confessions*. I would never seriously consider it as a career. Who was I trying to kid, pretending to be a proper temp?

Mr. Edson was frowning. He replaced the receiver.

"That was my sister-in-law, actually," he said. "The old man—Mr. Child, that's her father. He's quite elderly, and it seems he's had a bit of an accident."

"Oh," I said.

"Seems he went head-over-heels down a flight of steps. Nothing serious, fortunately, though his heart is a bit tricky. Everyone's gone to the hospital."

"Oh," I said.

He appeared almost bemused by the incident. "Well, I don't really think anyone will be in much before...oh, two or three this afternoon. If at all. You may as well go home, Carol."

"Do you want me to come back tomorrow?" I asked, uncertainly.

"Of course! Yes, of course. Can't do without you. Business is booming."

Mrs. Thatcher intercepted me with her purple mop-handle. "Where you going?"

"I'm leaving. The senior Mr. Child has met with dreaded misfortune, the children have gathered at his bedside, and I have been sent home."

"I knew it would happen one day," she said, her eyes bright. "I always said it would. All that miserliness finally done him in. Heart, was it?"

"He fell down the stairs."

Mrs. Thatcher grunted. "Dead, is he?"

"Lingering on, apparently."

"Better off dead than breathing at his age," she said, reaching into her apron pocket for her packet of cigarettes. "What with a son-in-law like Mr. Edson. Won't leave the ladies alone, that one. Not since his missus left him for a driving instructor. You'll want to be on your guard around him."

"I'll watch out," I promised.

"You mind you do, or I won't be responsible." She mopped her way down the hallway. "I won't," she called over her shoulder.

I climbed the steps to the rooftop garden. No need to leave just yet. The green park bench was hiding in the shade. I dragged it around to face the sun. The tomatoes and geraniums might enjoy my company for an hour or so.

With a guilty glance across the slate roofs and chimney pots of London, I switched on the radio I'd retrieved from the bottom drawer of Sandra's desk. I slipped the *True Confessions* out of my bag. And I flipped it open to the first sinful tale.

ABOUT TRUE CONFESSIONS...

I spent the summers of 1973 and 1974 working as a Temp for Brook Street Bureau in London, England. I had virtually no experience and no formal training in office procedures. I could type 60 wpm, however, which was all that really seemed to matter. One of my references was genuine, but I made up a second one, gambling that nobody in London was going to put through a phone call to Regina, Saskatchewan to check up on me.

The builders yard in this story was based on a real builders yard in Kensal Rise and the job is very similar to what I experienced during my two-week assignment there in 1974. There really was a rooftop garden with tomatoes and geraniums and a view of what turned out to be Wormwood Scrubs, with London in the very misty distance. Mrs. Thatcher, the tea lady, was borrowed from a different assignment—a lawnmower firm in Croydon—in 1973.

The story was originally published in *Green's Magazine,* a small literary journal in Regina, Saskatchewan, Volume XII, Number 4, Summer 1984.

4

CREATURES FROM GREEK MYTHOLOGY

I loved Miss Dionysus. A handsome woman, skin Mediterranean olive, hair sleek and black, she arrived from the Teachers' College shortly before Christmas 1970 and reduced my social life to shambles. The other boys might refer to her, in locker room acerbity, as Miss Dialysis. I, however, pledged to win her heart.

I was, at the time, fifteen years old.

"A dance," said my mother, who believed such things led to acts of unspeakable decadence. She had sent me to an all-male institution in the belief that I would forget all about women, and become a priest. She had forgotten about St. Mary's Academy for Girls, located across the street from my school.

"Don't worry," I said. "The priests have forewarned us that dancing leads to body contact, and that body contact leads to mortal sin."

"Matthew," said my mother.

"Anyway," I continued, "I have to go to this dance. The Pope has appointed me the official shoe-checker."

My mother smiled. "If you're checking shoes," she said, "you won't have time to dance."

"I knew you'd be pleased," I said.

With the arrival of Miss Dionysus, our social studies periods were thrown into chaos. Gone were the historical lectures on Greece and Rome, ancient civilizations, marauding armies, enlightened philosophies. Gone was the well-ordered structure wrought by thumb-creased notes and an equally worn, white-haired octogenarian priest.

The era of Socio-Economic Game-Set Simulations was upon us. Our desks became Seats of Power, the floor-markings political boundaries. It was time for me to prove my worth.

Elevated to a senior-ranking position in the army of a small Middle Eastern country, I impulsively, and with great letting of blood, overthrew the government. I accused Henry McIntyre - a large, greasy boy who ruled a neighbouring desk - of treaty violations. He retaliated by threatening to blow me up. Tempers quickened, and crazed fingers triggered dangerous buttons. I glowed with pride amid the nuclear devastation.

Miss Dionysus remained unimpressed.

Cast adrift in a colander lifeboat with the bedraggled victims of World War Eight, I tackled Survival by pitching the weakest overboard. Washed up on an uncharted island, I reverted to William Golding atrocities. Bloody assassinations and countless revolutions later, I emerged - the undisputed Leader of the World.

Miss Dionysus accused me, point blank, of non-co-operation.

I was in despair. My marks plummeted. I roasted in the hell-fires of disgrace.

My only hope of redemption lay in the Jesuit College Christmas Frolic.

Suave in my grey trousers and blue Jesuit blazer, I took my place behind the table with Henry McIntyre. Henry, who had also volunteered to check shoes, was resplendent in an extra-large Hamlet shirt, plaid Fortrel trousers with two-inch cuffs, and mismatched Argyle socks. Next door, in the gym, the band plodded through Jimi Hendrix. The lead guitarist was one of those I had consigned to the sharks during Simulated Lifeboat Week.

In vain, I searched for Miss Dionysus. She was nowhere to be seen.

I carried a pair of blue-stripe Adidas to the back of the hallway and presented their owner with a claim-tag.

"Oh my God," Henry panted, rubbing sweat from his dimpled hands. "There's Louise Wicijowski. The girl of my dreams!"

A flat-chested girl from St. Mary's was struggling with her sling-backs.

"She has the biggest tits in St. Mary's Academy! My sister *knows* her. She goes to pyjama parties. Oh God..."

I seized the sling-backs from the flat-chested girl and dumped them beside the blue-stripe Adidas.

Henry handed over the claim-slip.

"She has *showers* after Phys-Ed with her!"

———◇———

Our shift was over for the evening. I skirted the perimeter of the gymnasium, searching for the girl of *my* dreams. Where was she, my creature from Greek mythology? Probably in the Staff Room, smoking a cigarette. Deflated, I cruised the dance floor, hands jammed into my trouser pockets.

Why, I wondered, did these girls feel the need to stand in whole conventions, gossiping, combing their hair. Didn't they know how difficult it was for a lone male to saunter up and ask one of them to dance? They were like covered wagons, these virtuous females, drawn in a tight circle to protect their chaste campground from horseback heathens.

I passed the rolled-up tumbling mats, and nearly collided with Henry, who was happily guiding a large-breasted Sophomore across the basketball key. It was not Louise Wicijowski. Louise Wicijowski had turned him down flat. Undaunted, Henry had sought out another. As he galloped past me for the third time, I was overpowered by the half-bottle of Brut he had doused on himself ten minutes earlier.

In the mad-flash light of the flickering strobes, I wandered out of the gymnasium, disappointed.

Beyond the foyer and the Morality Squad chaperones lay the glazed-tile hallways of Jesuit College. Unseen, I slipped through the partitioning doors and meandered down the foot-worn steps to the basement.

The Staff Room lay beneath the ground, buried, a cubicle in the Labyrinth of Knossos. I stood before the frost-windowed door, my heart pounding. What would I say to her? What *could* I say to her? Would she like to dance? Would she like a cigarette? Cautiously, I raised my fist, and knocked.

There was no answer.

I knocked again, more loudly.

The gods were out; nobody was home.

I turned away from the door, distracted by a strange and magical Eastern scent. It was a woman. She wafted, rather than walked. She wore a long, patchwork skirt, and her hair swung down her back, caught up in a thick, braided rope. She was beautiful. And she looked decidedly different from the girls of St. Mary's Academy.

Curiously, I followed her around the corner. She disappeared into a classroom. I read the sign scotch-taped to the door. COMMUNITY COLLEGE. INTRODUCTION TO ART. PLEASE COME IN.

Inside, two bearded youths squatted over electric potters' wheels, spinning urns from mud-wet clay. An intent group of elderly ladies sketched a still life: two withered oranges. a brown chair, a half-empty bottle of wine and a human skull, cracked. And at a bespattered work table in the centre of the room sat the woman with the rope-braid hair, daubing watercolour rainbows on her eyelids.

"Hi," she said, looking up at me. "Did you come from the dance?"

I nodded.

"This is your school?"

I nodded again.

"Far out. Hey - do you have any rosaries on you?"

I laughed. "Sorry," I said. "Just my hair shirt and birch twigs tonight."

She laughed with me. "Only, I really dig rosaries, you know? I used to have one that belonged to a nun...only the beads were so big I got bruises when I walked. All down my front."

She indicated the area around her breasts.

"You're not supposed to wear rosaries around your neck," I said.

"Yeah," she grinned, "but they look really tacky hanging off my old man's rear-view mirror." She offered me the paintbrush. "Could you, like, do some heavy black eyelashes for me?"

I sat beside her, on a stool, and dipped the brush into a bottle of India ink.

"Anything for the lips?" I checked, finishing up. "A moustache, perhaps...?"

"Oh, wow. No...I like my lips to be natural...but we can do my nipples if you want."

"No thanks," I answered hastily. One of the potters looked up from his wheel, and smiled.

"Can I paint your face?" she asked.

"Another time, perhaps. I'm due back at the dance."

She would not, however, be dissuaded. "I can see you all done in lightning and thunder," she said, the rainbows animated. "All zig-zags and sparks."

"Really," I replied. "I'm more your sun, moon and stars type. Very placid. Very peaceful."

"Hey," she said. "Cosmic. I could do the whole astrological chart on your forehead! C'mon. What's your name?"

"Matthew," I said, extending my hand - and the paintbrush - with caution.

"Cynthia," she replied, accepting them both.

———◆———

Henry McIntyre squinted into my face. I had scrubbed away what remained of Pisces and Aquarius, but some red and orange Taurean streaks still persisted. Unabashed, I flicked my hair away from my forehead. I had nothing to be ashamed of.

Drawing me aside, still eyeing the strange paint, Henry shared his dreadful discovery.

"No!" I shouted, horror-struck.

"I'm telling you - she's engaged. She came up here and *told* me. Miss Dialysis is engaged!"

"No," I said, more belatedly.

"She says she's going to move to Australia and educate the masses Down Under. She just got proposed-to tonight. That's why she was late."

"Oh, God," I wailed.

"God does not exist, Matthew," Henry reminded me, boldly.

"If God did exist," I said, "I would pray immediately to him for personal intervention. Another woman...to lure her man away...an incurable disease..."

"Leprosy," said Henry.

"Whispered pleadings." I lowered my voice in cruel imitation of my beloved's intended. "My little Greek figlet, you must abandon me...you must stay at Jesuit for the remainder of the school year...and live your life to its fullest..."

"Take my finger as a souvenir," said Henry.

I looked at him. "I wonder if they engage in premarital sex."

"They'd have to confess it," Henry reasoned. "'Bless me, father, for I have sinned, we have grievously fornicated eight times this week...'"

"Eight?"

"Three times on Saturday."

"What about Sunday?"

"She wouldn't dare," said Henry. "Miss Dialysis is much too devout for that."

"If she was so devout," I said, miserably, "she'd stay here and finish teaching us, instead of charging halfway around the world to waste Simulation Nuclear Holocaust on heathen Australians."

"Who are you phoning, Matthew?"

I replaced the receiver, and looked at my mother. "That's really none of your business," I said.

"All right," she replied, although she continued to dust in the hallway, and made no attempt to give me privacy.

I took the telephone into the bathroom and shut the door. I climbed into the tub, and redialled Cynthia's number. Out in the hallway, my mother had paused again in her cleaning, and was lingering by the bathroom door. I reached across and flushed the toilet.

"Hi man, who's this?"

"This is Matthew," I said.

"Far out. Hey - thanks for the rosary!"

"My mother will never miss it."

"What's that noise?"

"It's...the toilet."

"Are you in the can, Matthew?"

"No...I'm in the bath."

"Far out. Are you all bare naked?"

"No...I'm fully clothed. Actually."

"In the *bath*?"

"There's no water in it."

"Cosmic," Cynthia laughed. "Dry cleaning."

I swallowed hard. "The reason I called is...um...do you want to go to a movie? Or something?"

"Sure," she answered, easily.

"Oh God, what a relief."

"You're so weird, Matthew."

"I'll see you tomorrow night. I'll come by the school."

"Can I paint your face again?"

"Anytime," I said. "Venus and Mars. Thunder and lightning. Creatures from Greek mythology. Anything."

<hr />

Henry had been telling the truth; the wedding plans of Miss Dionysus went ahead as scheduled. She did not care about me, or the class. She cared only about Australia, and the man to whom she was engaged. The blissful couple even dared to appear at a Jesuit basketball game, hand in hand, radiantly happy, unconcerned that we were losing 84 to 13.

"The brazen hussy," said Henry, kicking the bleacher with his Hush-Puppy slip-ons.

"The nerve," I agreed.

"And a dentist, too. What taste in men."

"She'll always have perfect incisors," I echoed sadly.

My Social Studies suffered as my attention span withered. It was inevitable. I became less ruthless at the simulations, and spent my time instead dreaming of watercolour Leos and egg-tempera minotaurs. One day, lost in my labyrinth, I allowed Henry McIntyre to slaughter a desert full of guerrillas - of which I was the rebel leader.

My fate was sealed: I was removed from the game. I spent the remainder of the period drawing pictures of Icarus and Daedalus in my notebook, waxen feathers, brilliant sunshine and gently lapping waters.

In time, I knew, I would begin to refer to my teacher in disparaging terms. And after she had gone to Australia, and the white-haired old priest had restored calm and order to the classroom, I would gradually, if not sadly, only remember her as Miss Dialysis.

ABOUT CREATURES FROM GREEK MYTHOLOGY...

This was one of the first short stories I wrote after I moved to Vancouver in 1982. It has its roots in my own high school days at Central Collegiate in Regina, when I had a crush on my history teacher and there were Fine Arts students in the basement who really did paint rainbows on their faces and throw clay pots on wheels and there was a teacher who would draw a moustache in India ink above your upper lip if you dared to leave your paintbrush sitting in a jar of water. (Art was one of the subjects I excelled in at Central...other than the incident with the paintbrush.)

Central was non-denominational, but I knew all about Catholic schools—I'd attended Holy Rosary for my Kindergarten to Grade 8, and the nuns did their very best to convince me to stay in the system going forward.

I resisted.

At Central, you could get in free to school dances if you volunteered to check shoes. The reason shoes had to be checked was that the dances were held in the gym, and the gym had a very expensive floor which The Powers That Be were anxious to preserve in its pristine state. Therefore, shoes had to be removed—unless they were rubber-soled, but no one in their right mind wore sneakers to a school dance in the 1960s.

"Creatures from Greek Mythology" was the Second Prize Winner in the WQ Editors Prize competition, and was published in *Cross-Canada Writers Quarterly.* Vol 6, No. 1, 1984.

5

THE MAN IN THE GREY ELDORADO

It was a sizzler. Thirty-two Celsius. Ozzie trudged around to the front of the house, heaved his box of textbooks into the back of his pickup, climbed into the cab and headed out to the school.

The Saskatchewan Arts Camp was seventy miles north of the city, in a former TB sanitorium. It shared the bottom of a shallow valley with a lake, two towns, and a meandering road that in less fortunate times had been the TB patients' only link to the healthy world beyond.

Since the onset of summer, the water in the lake had taken on the consistency of diluted pea soup. Ozzie wrinkled his nose as he drove into the valley. Prevailing westerlies. The diluted pea soup smelled like dead fish.

His room at the school was beside the entrance on the main floor of a two-storey pavilion which had once housed the sanitorium's nurses. It was noisy and suffocatingly hot for most of the day. The quiet, shady accommodations upstairs were reserved for the more prominent writing instructors.

Aside from some productions on local TV, a couple of plays produced by Little Theatre and four crassly commercial detective novels which were as forgettable as they were cliched, Ozzie Kimball's solitary claim to fame was a 48-minute episode of *The Man from UNCLE* two decades earlier. It was an interesting little story about the RCMP, a farmer's daughter and a top-secret THRUSH outpost disguised as an abandoned flour mill on the outskirts of Moose Jaw. Of course, Moose Jaw had never actually been mentioned in the story. The suspect building was identified only by an Establishing Shot appropriately labelled *Somewhere in Canada*.

It had been twenty years since Ozzie's claim to fame, and try as he might, he could not persuade anybody to remember him for anything else. It was never "Ozzie Kimball, whose latest drama, *Canola Calling* can be seen this Saturday on Community Cable 10." No. It was always "Ozzie Kimball, author of *The Farina Affair*, one of the last episodes of *The Man from UNCLE* to be aired before the series was abruptly cancelled in January 1968." Ozzie did not feel this was fair at all.

He was contemplating just how *un*fair it was as he lugged his box of textbooks into the pavilion. A fresh stack of scripts from the students in his screenplay workshop was waiting on the floor outside his room. He unlocked the door and carried the scripts and his box inside. He shut the door behind him and, feeling the effects of the hot prairie afternoon, the long drive from the city and a rather late party the night before, stretched out on his squeaky hospital bed to contemplate the smattering of fish-fly corpses in the saucer of the glass lampshade screwed into the ceiling.

It was about half an hour later that Benny knocked on the door. Benny was a big kid with long black frizzy hair and a strong desire to rewrite *Chinatown* as a comedy.

"What?" Ozzie hollered.

"Some guy down at the Main Office wants your autograph."

"Me?" said Ozzie, sitting up. "Some guy wants *my* autograph? Nah, Benny—he's got me mistaken for Jerry. Go get Jerry. He's the famous author. "

"Nope," said Benny, through the closed door. "Nope -it's you he wants, Ozzie. He looks like a real big shot, too. He's driving a real classy car. "

"Okay," he said, sighing. "Okay." As they were walking together down the wooden walkway, he added: "If this is about that fucking U. N. C. L. E. script, I'll puke."

Benny disappeared into the duplicating room, and Ozzie approached the main gate by himself. He could see the classy car Benny had described, glinting in the sunlight. It was a Cadillac, grey, with tinted windows and spoke wheels. Its driver was standing in the gravel with his legs apart and 4 his arms folded. He was about fifty, and was oozing sweat. He was wearing sunglasses.

"Hello," Ozzie said, extending his hand. "I'm Ozzie Kimball."

"*Oscar* Kimball?" the man checked.

"Yeah."

The man glanced down at an article torn from the local newspaper. It was a review of *Canola Calling* and a brief biography of the author. There was a picture of Ozzie at the top of the column.

"That's Oscar Kimball too," said Ozzie.

"Been writing this kinda stuff for a while?"

"Well, yes, a number of years..."

"And spy stories too? On television?"

"I knew it," said Ozzie. "Jesus Christ. You guys just won't leave it alone, will you? That was twenty fucking years ago. Can't you give a guy credit for *progress*?"

The man said nothing. He simply stared at Ozzie. Ozzie could see his reflection in the sunglasses.

"You want my autograph?" he said.

"I want you to get into the car, Mr. Kimball."

"What for?"

"We're going for a little ride, you and me. We have some things to discuss."

"*The Man from U.N.C.L.E.*? You wanna discuss *The Man from U. N.C.L.E.*? Forget it, pal. I have a class in half an hour. Try sending a fan letter to NBC. Maybe you'll get an autographed picture of Napoleon Solo or something."

He whipped around, and headed back across the visitors' parking lot, cursing The United Network Command for Law and Enforcement, and all it stood for. He could hear the man in the sunglasses hurrying to catch up behind him. His shoes were going KA-CHING, KA-CHING, KA-CHING in the loose gravel.

"Hold it, Kimball!" he said.

Ozzie kept walking. The man caught up to him, slightly out of breath.

"I'd advise you to cooperate. "

Ozzie froze as something hard jabbed him in the small of his back.

"Now, turn around, Mr. Kimball. Nice and slow. "

Ozzie turned. The revolver ascended to his left nostril.

"Is this legal in Canada?" he said.

The man did not reply. He guided Ozzie towards the car. He opened the door, and sat Ozzie down inside. If Ozzie had been Napoleon Solo, he would have jumped out and run like hell while the man unlocked the driver's side. Of course, if Ozzie had been Napoleon Solo, he would have decked the guy with a well-aimed slice to the back of the neck at the first hint of trouble. Rut that was television. This was Saskatchewan.

"Nice Continental," he said, instead, patting the leather seat.

"It's an Eldorado," the man answered, with a snarl. He started the engine. A little bell went PONG PONG PONG somewhere inside the dashboard. Ozzie looked up, startled.

There was a tiny notice affixed to the glove compartment; it said: DON'T BE CAUGHT DEAD SITTING ON YOUR SEATBELT.

Ozzie buckled up.

They headed down the road towards Milton, the larger of the two valley towns. The review of Ozzie's play sat on the seat between them. Dear Fan: This is Ozzie Kimball. *The Farina Affair*. Married, with two teenaged kids. Owns his own house. Is allergic to cats.

"You know," said Ozzie, "someone' s going to notice I'm gone. Benny. Benny'll notice."

"Nobody will notice," said the man. "I took the liberty of checking your schedule. You told me a lie, Mr. Kimball. Your class is not until this evening."

"What, exactly, do you want?" Ozzie asked. "I mean, seriously? Illya Kuryakin's middle name? Napoleon Solo's astrological sign? What?"

The man's lips twitched. It might have been a smile. As they rode up over the crest of a hill, Ozzie had a grand view of the lake, vile green in the afternoon sun.

Uncontrollably, he began to contemplate his otherwise undistinguished life. He wondered...would he ever see his '52 pickup again...?

———•◦•———

The hotel in Milton didn't merit a name—just a rusted CANADA DRY sign, squeaking lazily over the entrance to the bar. The man with the sunglasses motioned Ozzie inside.

"Buy you a round of draft?" Ozzie quipped, lamely, as the smell of warm beer and cigarette smoke greeted them.

"Cut out the funny stuff and head for the can."

Ozzie did as he was told. The only other person in the men's washroom was leaning up against the wall, staring morosely into the bottom of a urinal.

"He your sidekick?" Ozzie asked.

As if on queue, the second man straightened up, and pushed open the door to the single cubicle. OUT OF ORDER had been scribbled onto a paper serviette and Scotch-taped to the pock-marked paint.

"After you, Mr. Kimball. "

"Ha ha," Ozzie said, nervously, laughing. "Isn't this kinda weird, fellas? I mean, a joke is a joke…"

"Mr. Kimball," said the man in the sunglasses. "I assure you. This is no joke. It's taken us twenty years to find you. You will now do us the honour of stepping into the cubicle." He waved the gun in Ozzie's face.

"Jesus Christ," said Ozzie. "Who *are* you guys?"

"All in good time, Mr. Kimball."

The two men followed him in, and the sidekick pressed a screw on the side of the Onliwon paper dispenser. There was a soft whirring noise, and then a click, as if machinery was falling into place.

"Flush," said the man with the sunglasses.

"Eh?"

"Flush."

Ozzie flushed. It was one of those handles he really had to lean on. He gave it his best shot. Immediately, the walls began to stretch, and he was hurled onto the toilet seat. Down, they sank, down, at an incredible speed, down, into the bowels of Saskatchewan. The cubicle screeched to a stop as rapidly as it had accelerated. The door sprang open. Ozzie peered out, unbelieving. Here, hundreds of feet beneath the Qu'Appelle Valley, was a hidden complex, a secret institution. Men and women marched briskly about their business through white, antiseptic corridors.

He was escorted out of the cubicle to a desk, which was littered with pamphlets and scraps of paper; a Saskatchewan Government Telephone Directory; three staplers; a bottle of correcting fluid; and a booklet describing the Canada Council's Explorations Program. Behind the desk sat a beautiful woman.

"Mr. Kimball will be our guest for the next few hours," said the sidekick, who was beginning to remind Ozzie more and more of Starsky, or Hutch—he couldn't remember which was which.

Of course," the beautiful woman murmured. She withdrew three peel-off stickers from a file folder on her desk.

HELLO (they said)
MY NAME IS...

"Aw, come on," said Ozzie. "Even Napoleon and Illya got proper badges. 2 and 11. Remember?"

"This is not U.N.C.L.E.!" the sidekick hissed.

"A matter of funding," added the man in the sunglasses. "We've found it necessary to cut down on the frills. ID buttons were the first to go." He looked pained. "No matter. Come this way, Mr. Kimball."

Ozzie was escorted down one of the cold white hallways, and into a room. The room contained a couch and some chairs, a circular table with a globe in the middle of it, and a television screen, beneath which was an array of dials and knobs and flashing lights.

"You kidnap Mr. Waverly's decorator too?" Ozzie asked, as he was pushed into the nearest chair. It turned out to be the kind that swivelled, and he was whipped around by the man in the sunglasses before he could make any more clever comments.

"Now then," said the man, leaning over Ozzie, so that Ozzie could smell his breath—Cinnamon Tic-Tacs. "How, exactly, did you find out about our Moose Jaw operations?"

"Eh?"

"Come on, Mr. Kimball. Don't play games. You wrote a script about a nuclear power plant in an abandoned flour mill in Moose Jaw. Who was your contact?"

"Jesus Christ!" said Ozzie, growing more and more frustrated. "That was fiction! Can't a guy have a little imagination? I mean, come on. Who'd be dumb enough to operate a spy network out of *Saskatchewan*?"

The man with the sunglasses looked visibly insulted.

"We would, Mr. Kimball," he answered, with a stiff smile.

"Jeez," said Ozzie. "I'm sorry."

"Sorry is just not good enough, Mr. Kimball. Your little escapade jeopardized six years of planning, millions of dollars and thousands of man hours of work. You effectively rendered our plant inoperative, and we were forced, as a result, to dismantle and relocate. Needless to say, my superiors were not amused. Mr. Kimball—you managed, single-handedly, to destroy our entire North American operations centre. "

"And it took you twenty years to track me down just to tell me?" Ozzie said, incredulous. "Boy, are you efficient."

The sidekick exchanged glances with the man in the sunglasses, and then leaned down over the chair. "Your informant was a double-agent. We want to know who he—or she—was."

"I told you," Ozzie said, getting to his feet impatiently. "I made it up. Understand?"

The man in the sunglasses shoved Ozzie back into the chair. Bewildered, Ozzie tapped the side of his head with his finger.

"Honest! It came out of here. I don't know anything about any spy organizations. I was just trying to make a buck. I thought up a plot, sold the script, and got paid. That was that. End of story. "

The man in the sunglasses looked across at his sidekick. Starsky, Ozzie decided.

"He's obviously been paid off to keep quiet. This is gonna be a little tougher than we thought. "

"Who *are* you guys?" said Ozzie, exasperated.

The two men ignored him. "We'll have to rely on more persuasive methods."

"Great," said Ozzie, throwing up his hands. "Bamboo shoots? Wine presses? Wait—don't tell me. You're going to lock me in a room with a large gong and bang it until I'm driven insane by the noise."

The sidekick gave him a disparaging glance.

"Really, Mr. Kimball," said the man in the sunglasses.

"Let's take our friend next door, shall we?"

Next door was a cell-like room, with dull grey walls and a concrete floor. There was a chair in the centre of the room, and a wardrobe against the wall. The wardrobe was fitted with a full-length mirror. Ozzie was deposited in the chair, and his hands were tied around his back with rope.

"You're going to dissolve me with devious anti-matter foam?" he guessed.

"You've been watching too much TV," answered the sidekick. With obvious calculation, he walked over to the cupboard. The door creaked open. As it swung past, Ozzie saw his reflection—mirrored, confused...and defiant! Yes, defiant! These guys were crazy! These guys were insane! If he ever managed to escape, the first thing he was going to do was put them in a script. A TV-movie! For NBC! CBS! Satellite!

"Miaow."

"Eh?" Ozzie looked down.

"Miaow."

By the wardrobe sat a cat. It was the biggest cat Ozzie had ever seen.

Another cat leaped out of the cupboard. It was a tabby. It was followed by a third...and a fourth...a fifth...

"Oh, shit," said Ozzie.

Cats swarmed all over the floor, purring, romping, rubbing up against each other, braiding themselves between Ozzie's legs and licking his toes between the leather straps of his sandals.

"Get away!" he shouted, as a kitten dug its claws into his ankle. He kicked it off. Already, he could feel the membranes in his nose beginning to swell; his sinuses were going wild; his throat was closing up.

Another animal, a great tiger-striped alley cat—leaped into Ozzie's lap and began to purr and tread its paws into his thigh.

"Get off me!" Ozzie croaked.

"*Prreow*?"

"You guys! I can't breathe!"

"Tell us who your contact was."

"I'm fucking suffocating and you wanna know about goddamn flour mills? You guys are nuts!"

"Let's leave him in here for a while," the sidekick suggested. "He'll loosen up."

The man in the sunglasses flashed a grin, and left. The sidekick closed the cupboard door and turned around. He had to get past Ozzie to reach the exit. In a split second, Ozzie was ready. As he crossed his path, Ozzie raised both legs and shot his feet into the sidekick's stomach. He staggered back, but it was not enough to knock him over. The look of surprise on the sidekick's face said it all. Oh boy, thought Ozzie. Here it comes.

"I wish you hadn't done that, Mr. Kimball," wheezed the sidekick, straightening up. He lunged towards Ozzie, fists balled.

Instinctively, Ozzie shut his eyes and screwed up his face. But the blow never came. Instead, there was an unholy screech—and he opened his eyes just in time to see the great tiger-striped alley cat shoot out from under the sidekick's left foot, tail fluffed and teeth bared.

Thinking fast, Ollie booted the guy in the nuts.

"Bet you never saw that on *U.N.C.L.E.*," he said, as the sidekick flew backwards and crunched into the wardrobe. The mirror cracked; shards of glass crashed to the concrete floor. The heavy piece of furniture trembled, rocking on two corners as Ollie's victim groped for a hand-hold.

Ozzie held his breath. The wardrobe rocked, and then toppled, pinning the sidekick underneath, decidedly unconscious. If only I had something to cut through these ropes, Ozzie thought, as every single Napoleonic escape rushed through his mind. Miniature chain saws in heels of shoes? Detonators in tie-pins? He looked down. He wasn't wearing a tie. He was barely wearing a shirt.

A piece of glass from the shattered mirror glinted on the floor. Clever. But he couldn't reach it, not even by shuffling forward on the chair. The sidekick's head was in the way.

But the sidekick's—Starsky's—mouth was open.

Cautiously, Ozzie scuffed the chair across the floor.

He manoeuvred around, crossed his fingers, and kicked backwards. The chair tipped, and for a split second he hovered midway, feet dangling, eyes fixed to the ceiling.

And then, he fell.

Ozzie could tell by the warm dampness surrounding his fingers that his hands were in the man's mouth.

Triumphantly, he employed the sidekick's teeth to cut the ropes.

Ten minutes later, Ozzie was a free man. With great caution, he opened the door, and peered out into the hallway. Damn. The man with the sunglasses was doing sentry duty. Well...if he could just slip out...and sprint the other way...he looked behind him, at the toppled wardrobe and the coven of cats. The sidekick was coming around. Ozzie had no choice; he would have to move, fast.

He took a deep breath, and leaped out, skidding sideways as his rubber soles slipped on the shiny linoleum.

The man in the sunglasses whirled around, and the chase was on. Left ...right...Ozzie's sandals flapped in the corridor as all hell broke loose. Lights flashed and horns blared and security doors began to crash down around him.

He skidded around a corner. Dead end! There was nowhere to go! Frantically, he grabbed the nearest door handle. It gave, and Ozzie found himself in a kind of narrow hallway that sloped away and up. An emergency escape tunnel!

Mustering his last pool of energy, Ozzie scrambled through the darkness.

At last he reached the top, and kicked open a door. He broke into the night air, aware of voices and footsteps behind him. There was an old Ford parked in the ditch; the keys were in the ignition; Ozzie threw himself into the front and gunned the engine. He careened away from the town of Milton as flashes of lightning flickered in distant thunderheads, and the last of the sun sank down behind the hills of the Qu'Appelle Valley.

Sixty...seventy...eighty miles an hour. His ears popped as he careened down a hill into the valley. The white, comforting gleam of Arts Camp was just ahead; he skidded off the road and roared up the gravel access lane to the back of his pavilion. The car came to a stop in a cloud of dust, and Ozzie leaped out.

"*Help*!" he hollered, flying into the pavilion. "*Help*! You guys! Hide me! Save me!"

Where the hell were they? Not even the clatter of one decrepit typewriter answered his cries.

Where were they? *Outside*! Up on the hill! The evening workshop! It was outside!

Ozzie flapped down the hallway again, and cut out through the back door, and scrambled up into the scrub grass and sand.

"*Help*!" he screamed, grappling with the brittle weeds. His fingers sank into the hillside. Thistles spiked his toes. "Jesus Christ! Save me! "

Up above, he could make out about forty kids, gathered around an open fire, discussing technique with Jerry, the famous novelist.

"They wanna murder me!" Ozzie choked, falling forward into the flickering circle of light. "Call the police! Call the RCMP! Call U.N.C.L.E.! The spies are after me! "

"Who?" said Benny, leaning over to peer into Ozzie's ravaged face.

"The man in the grey Eldorado!" Ozzie spluttered. "Starsky and Hutch! Three hundred cats!"

Benny stared down the hill.

"Where?" he said.

Ozzie looked.

Nothing.

"They're hiding," he said.

Jerry let out a sympathetic laugh. "Living out your fantasies again, Kimball?"

"I tell you, they were there!"

"And where did these...spies...appear from?"

"They took me to Milton! There's a secret complex under the Canada Dry Hotel. You go into the men's can and you press Onliwon and you flush the toilet and then you go down—"

A snicker rose from the circle of writers. It grew into a vast, uproarious chuckle. It exploded. Benny fell to the ground, clutching his side, rolling in the dust. Jerry turned his back on Ozzie, and Ozzie saw his shoulders start to shake.

"Think we could make a sitcom out of it?" somebody asked, under their breath.

"All right!" Ozzie shouted. "Laugh! Go ahead! You'll see! It took them twenty years to find me! Tonight, when I'm dragged out of my bed and hauled back to Milton—to those cats—you'll see!"

Benny was steering him gently down the hill. He propelled Ozzie into the pavilion, and into his room. Ozzie was dazed by what he saw. Scraps of paper littered the floor. Sheets and blankets were twisted around the metal legs of the hospital bed. The top drawer in the dresser had been splintered.

"Jesus," said Ozzie.

"Musta been some dream," Benny answered. "Looks like you kinda kicked that drawer in your sleep or something."

"How do you know *they* didn't do that?"

"There was nobody here, Ozzie. You were asleep all afternoon. I banged on your door just before the workshop, and you never answered, so we just figured we'd let you dream on. You looked kinda tired earlier. I gotta get back to the class. See you later."

Benny left.

Ozzie looked at his foot. The big toe was three times its normal size, and was rimmed with dark, dried blood.

"It wasn't a dream," he said.

He sat for a few moments in the darkness, while Benny cleared up some of the paper. He sat rigid, on the edge of the bed, as the lightning flickered closer to the line of hills secluding the valley.

"It wasn't a dream," he said, again, but less sure this time. He had been sleepy...and it was hot...

Behind the pavilion, a car crunched down the lane. It was one of those quiet engines, the kind a Cadillac has. Ozzie absently picked a piece of dead skin off his hand. There were other, drying flakes, making a curious kind of circle around his wrist. Both wrists.

The car stopped, with its engine running, and a door slammed. Quiet footsteps approached the pavilion.

Ozzie stared at his left hand. In the band of his watch was a frayed strand of rope, intertwined with what looked like a single white whisker from a cat.

"It wasn't a dream," he said a third, and final, time, as the footsteps reached his door.

ABOUT THE MAN IN THE GREY ELDORADO...

The first draft of "The Man in the Grey Eldorado" was written round-about 1977 or 1978, and was inspired by a glorious few weeks I'd once spent at the Saskatchewan Summer School of the Arts (located in a former tuberculosis sanitorium near Fort Qu'Appelle).

The story was also inspired by my love of the tongue-in-cheek tv series from the 1960s, *The Man from U.N.C.L.E.* It isn't the only time that *U.N.C.L.E.* has informed my writing—my first novel, *Skywatcher,* was actually about a guy who played a spy on tv in the 1960s, as was its sequel, *The Cilla Rose Affair.* But this tale predates *Skywatcher* by about a dozen years.

"The Man in the Grey Eldorado" is one of two previously unpublished stories in this collection.

6

HERD MAINTENANCE

I once had a job that required me to be concerned about cows.

> Our file No. 500.5
> 07 July 1981
>
> Dear (   ),
> The Herd Maintenance Assistance Program Review Board has reviewed your application as a result of your appeal to have your eligible herd size increased.
>
> The Board has upheld your appeal and your application has been resubmitted for processing. This re-processing may result in either an assistance payment or rejection under other program criteria. You will be advised of the results.
>
> Yours truly,
> A. Zinkowski
> Co-ordinator
> Herd Maintenance Assistance Program
> AZ/wk

The men in this Department wear suits and ties and occupy all of the supervisory positions. They have private offices with windows and go downstairs for coffee in small groups of three and four.

The women are clerk-typists and occupy small corrals made out of orange padding in the middle of the floor.

Women from the same Department are not allowed to go for coffee together.

Because of the lack of available windows, I must go into the women's washroom to see what the weather is like. The window is high on the wall and I have to climb onto the counter containing the sinks and then stand on my toes in order to look Outside.

It is sunny today but there are clouds gathering on the horizon.

The other women in the Department are concerned about my obsession with the Outside, and do their best to avoid me.

I return to my little corral and punch three holes into the carbon copy of the memo I typed, then place the yellow sheet of paper into a binder on a shelf above my desk.

Perhaps I will now peruse an official pamphlet while I await the arrival of my next item of correspondence.

Alfalfa Production in Western Canada.

Maintenance of Community Pastureland.

This looks promising: *Stock-Poisoning Weeds of the West.*

Our file No. 501.5
07 July 1981

Dear (   ),
Your appeal to have your milk cows redesignated as dairy cattle has been upheld by the Herd Maintenance Assistance Program Review Board. A supplementary assistance payment will be issued to you in the near future.

Yours truly,
A. Zinkowski
Co-ordinator
Herd Maintenance Assistance Program
AZ/wk

A crisis has arisen. A husband and wife have both claimed assistance for the same herd of livestock, each filing separate applications. My supervisor has spent the last half hour shouting on the telephone.

I imagine the man and his wife standing side-by-side in a field filled with Holsteins. They each hold an official letter from my supervisor, demanding the return of one of the payments, or a reduction in the number of animals in each claim. A vertical red dotted line separates the couple, and also divides the herd into two equal parts, bisecting several individual and very startled-looking cows.

It is not good to cheat the Government, accidentally or otherwise.

In the cubicle beside the photocopier, there is a Ritual of Leaving underway. One of our number has decided to reproduce, and today is her last in the Department. The conversation ranges from husbands to babies, with mortgages thrown in for variety. They have collected money for a special gift: a bracelet with her name engraved upon it.

An identity at last.

I avoid the Ritual of Leaving, as I am only a Temp. I have applied for a transfer to the Department of Regional and Economic Expansion. At DREE, they prepare memos concerning Community Complexes. Somewhere in Saskatchewan, an entire town is suffering from the ravages of feeling inferior.

Soon, it will be time for lunch. Perhaps, this afternoon, I will photocopy the palms of my hands.

I have often wondered what would happen if I set the machine to 1,000 and disappeared. Will someone else come along and replace the paper when it runs out, and press the button to continue the copying?

Recently, a memo was circulated concerning the photocopier. It has been noted that, on several occasions, large quantities of yellow and pink circles from the three-hole punch have been found in the automatic paper feed. These have been rapidly distributed throughout the internal mechanisms of the machine, causing serious malfunctions and resulting in many lost hours of productive time and escalating repair costs.

The woman occupying the cubicle beside me eats the little paper circles which come out of the three-hole punch.

Our file No. 502.5
07 July 1981

Dear (   ),
The Herd Maintenance Assistance Program Review
Board has reviewed your application as a result of your
appeal against your rejection on the basis of crop yield.

The Board has upheld your appeal and your application
has been resubmitted for processing. This re-processing
may result in either an assistance payment or rejection
under other program criteria. You will be advised of the
results.

Yours truly,
A. Zinkowski
Co-ordinator
Herd Maintenance Assistance Program
AZ/wk

There is a major crisis in the building. The smell of raw sewage is
infiltrating the floors. Departmental supervisors are in a panic. They rush
down to have coffee in groups of five and six. Phone calls fly between
Herd Maintenance and Public Works.

I have photocopied the palms of my hands and sent 18 of these to
DREE and 47 to Public Works. I have taken the opportunity to climb
onto the counter in the women's washroom and look Outside. I have
discovered that we are in the midst of a thunderstorm.

With my supervisor downstairs in the canteen debating the dangers of
raw sewage, I have resorted to making elaborate designs on yellow bond
paper with various bottles of correcting fluid. I have several shades at my
desk, and have titled my work "Liquid Paper in Three Colours, with Red
Pen."

The woman in the cubicle beside me has four colours, as pink is
Extra. I have considered jealousy as a reaction, but have rejected it as an
inappropriate response, since I have a Red Pilot Fineliner, and she does
not.

Meanwhile, a memo has arrived from Public Works.

Our file No. 606.2
07 July 1981

This will acknowledge that we are attempting to place the problem of the sewer gas smell under control. Our investigation has indicated a faulty sewer link connection in the basement. The faulty line runs from the canteen staff toilet facilities to the building drainage lines. Our search for the root of the problem has not been facilitated by the fact that we have had a changeover of office staff since the toilet facilities were installed.

Our plan of action is as follows:
1) Ensure the basement drain taps are properly sealed at all times with water, also disinfectant as needed;
2) Arrange for a contract to correct the situation as soon as plans and specifications can be prepared and tenders called. This involves a sewage lift station to carry the waste to ceiling height sewage drains in the basement rather than trenching to the other side of the building.

I realize the health hazard involved but please be assured we have taken urgent steps to permanently remedy the situation and to eliminate any interim harmful effect.

G. Williams
Property Manager

I have made 147 copies and put them in my Out Tray to be delivered to the supervisor in charge of Community Complexes at DREE.

The men have returned from the canteen, and are now busily making phone calls to confirm their conclusions.

Tomorrow, when I type my letters, perhaps I will omit my initials from the lower left-hand corner. My supervisor's supervisor will not be able to tell who prepared the correspondence. Anarchy is in the air.

Our file No. 500.4
07 July 1981

Dear (   ),
The Herd Maintenance Assistance Program Review
Board has recommended that the township in which your
wintering area is located be included in the severe drought
area. Accordingly, we will resume processing of your application.

This processing may result in either an assistance payment
or rejection under other program criteria. You will be advised of the results.

A. Zinkowski
Co-ordinator
Herd Maintenance Assistance Program
AZ/

We are being sent home because of the fumes. The union has advised
us that they constitute a health hazard. Some of the supervisors have
elected to stay on the job. We will not lose any pay as a result of this action.

I have switched off my IBM Selectric, indicating that I am no longer
Here. Tomorrow morning, I will not switch it on again until I have
rearranged the pens in the top drawer of my desk.

On my way out, I pass the photocopying room.

I pause at the copier and remove an envelope from my pocket. I pull
open the paper tray and pour in the contents of the envelope. I slide it
shut again.

A recent federal study has concluded that padded cubicles are well
tolerated by most office workers in large, impersonal settings.

Soon, I will be transferred to DREE, on the 14th Floor.

I will no longer need to be concerned about cows.

ABOUT HERD MAINTENANCE...

I wrote "Herd Maintenance" in 1981 while I was working as a Temp at a federal government office in Regina.

This is the second unpublished story in the collection, although it did enjoy a brief life as a short, unproduced film script while I was at Vancouver Film School in 2003-4.

The script was a comedy, and had very little in common with the short story—other than its title, A. Zinkowski, the women who share the office with our nameless temp (in the film script she's called "Clara"), and the red dotted line bisecting the herd of cows.

The letters are real. The names have been removed to protect the innocent.

7

PERHAPS AN ANGEL

It was a bit frightening at first, sharing a life with someone who was born in 1791.

But once Mr. Deeley had acquainted himself with twenty-first century plumbing, and the fact that cooking a meal did not involve hanging a large iron pot over the fire in the sitting room, everything else was easy.

He was adapting well, Charlie thought, as she tidied up her desk at the Stoneford Village Museum, where she worked as a Historical Guide and Interpreter.

She glanced out of the window, which overlooked the garden—the museum was housed in what had once been the St. Eligius Vicarage, and her desk was in the kitchen. There was Mr. Deeley now, taking pictures of the exterior displays with her phone. Rather handsome, she had to admit. With long dark hair, and the most expressive fingers. Not particularly muscular, but nicely proportioned. Slightly taller than average height—which, in the time he'd come from, had actually been considered quite tall indeed.

A quick learner. And not afraid of anything new.

Not afraid of anything, really.

This character trait had served him well one month earlier, when he'd made the journey from 1825 to now.

Charlie went out through the back door to join Mr. Deeley by the village's whipping post.

"I recall this," he said thoughtfully. "However, in my recollection, it did not reside in the vicar's garden."

"Your memory's correct," Charlie said. "It was originally at the top end of the Village Green. It was moved here in the 1970s to preserve it.

Drunken yobs coming out of The Dog's Watch had a habit of using it as a public toilet."

"But it is still in use as originally intended?" Mr. Deeley asked, slightly confused.

"Thankfully not," Charlie replied. "We're much more enlightened these days, Mr. Deeley. We sentence drunken yobs to community payback. We've got two of them repainting the Village Hall as we speak."

She took her phone back, popping it into her bag.

"We've got a tent over on the green with a jolly display about crime and punishment through the ages," she said. "Natalie's idea to attract more visitors to the museum. Blood and gore are far more interesting than a broken medieval cooking pot discovered under a parking lot. Come on, it's time you were introduced."

• ◦ •

The Village Green was in the midst of hosting Stoneford's annual summer fair, an August ritual. Charlie could remember the days, in her childhood, when the fair had involved merry-go-rounds and bumper cars, Ferris wheels and funhouses and stalls offering stuffed toys as prizes for contests that few ever seemed able to win.

The Stoneford summer fair these days was a much less exciting, and far less populated, event. There was a dog show, and a bouncy pirate ship for the kids. Stalls had been set up, but instead of ring-tosses and shooting contests, they hawked used DVDs and trinkets and jars of pickles and preserves from local farms. A portrait artist had been borrowed from the next village over, along with someone who did manicures and pedicures and foot massages.

In the past that Charlie remembered, the Village Green had been crammed with stalls and attractions—and fairgoers. It had been such a busy place that she'd never been able to understand how it had all fit into the little triangle of land at Stoneford's heart. Indeed, the day after the merry-go-rounds, bumper cars and Ferris wheels had packed up and motored away, and the stalls had been dismantled, she'd always made a point of going back to the green to try and imagine how it had all been laid out. And every year, it still didn't make any sense.

Nowadays, it was easy to see, because there were enormous gaps everywhere.

One of the local cafes was offering takeaway snacks from a tent near the low stone wall at the green's western edge. Charlie bought two sausage rolls and shared them with Mr. Deeley. They wandered across to the ancient Village Oak, where a booth had been set up endeavouring to Save the Hedgehogs.

"Save the Hedgehogs," Charlie mused. "Remember, Mr. Deeley? That was how we first met in 1825. I was standing underneath this lovely old tree after discovering that my mobile still worked—and you popped up out of nowhere and I nearly had a heart attack. I told you I was looking for hedgehogs! And you very kindly showed me a family of them having a little meal in the moonlight, under some bushes."

"I did not 'pop up out of nowhere', Mrs. Collins," Mr. Deeley replied, easily. "I had, in fact, been observing you for some minutes, and was intrigued by the device you held in your hand—in spite of your attempt to conceal it from me—and the fact that you seemed to be muttering to yourself for no apparent reason."

Next to the hedgehog booth was the museum tent, where Natalie's graphic punishment photos competed with the supercute pictures of spiny baby Eulipotyphlas for fairgoers' attention.

"I was not 'muttering to myself'," Charlie countered, just as easily. "I was sending a text to my cousin. And I had no idea you'd been watching me. You never said a word about seeing my mobile."

"Muttering to Nick, then," Mr. Deeley teased. "I preferred to remain in the dark."

Charlie looked at him, and laughed. "I do love you," she said.

Mr. Deeley smiled.

To the north of the Village Oak, near the top end of the green and within sight of The Dog's Watch Inn, one of those contraptions had been set up where you threw a ball at a target and, if your eye was good and your aim true, you ended up dunking whoever was sitting on the spring-loaded bench into a pool of freezing cold water.

This afternoon, it was Reg Ferryman, the Inn's proprietor.

The queue for the booth stretched all the way to the low stone wall—it was easily the most popular attraction of the fair.

And there, on the eastern edge of the green, off by itself, was an unusual-looking tent, eight-sided, its conical roof a glorious purple, its wall panels sheer scarlet and lilac, its posts striped candy-cane red and white. The front panels had been tied back, and inside sat a Gypsy fortune teller.

"A thought for your pennies?" she inquired, as Charlie and Mr. Deeley walked past.

The woman was elderly, with flowing grey hair, and was dressed in a loose white blouse and long summer skirt. Golden bangles dripped from her wrists and ears, and she wore many rings on her fingers. Mr. Deeley stopped and stared at her.

"I know you," he said. "You are Esmerelda, of the New Forest Gypsies. I have conversed with you before, on this same Village Green."

"She couldn't be," Charlie said quietly. "And you couldn't have, Mr. Deeley..."

"The *gorgio* is correct," the Gypsy woman replied. "We are previously acquainted." She turned to Charlie. "Your companion is not of this time. Will you come inside?"

Charlie looked at Mr. Deeley.

"Do you trust her?"

"With my life," Mr. Deeley replied.

------◄○►------

"The Tarot," Esmerelda said, placing a deck face down on the table-cloth. "It is familiar to you?"

"I know of the Tarot, yes," Charlie said. "But I don't pretend to understand it."

"What is your question?"

Charlie looked at Mr. Deeley, and then at Esmerelda.

"I don't have any questions," she said. "And I have to tell you, I'm very much a skeptic..."

"We all have questions, *gadji*. Think. What is it you wish most to know in this life?"

Charlie thought for a moment, then glanced again at Mr. Deeley and smiled. "Shall I tell you what it is?"

Esmerelda shrugged. "It is not necessary. The cards will provide your answer, whether you ask it aloud, or keep it to yourself. The choice is yours."

"Then I think I'd like to keep it to myself."

"Shuffle the deck."

Charlie gave her half-eaten sausage roll to Mr. Deeley, and shuffled the cards awkwardly. She'd never got the hang of doing it properly, and envied those who could make it look effortless. And this deck was ancient, its cards' edges rough and frayed.

"Now with your left hand, cut the deck. Three times."

Charlie did so, stacking the result neatly on the cloth.

"Choose one."

Charlie picked a card from the middle of the deck, and handed it, face down, to Esmerelda.

Esmerelda turned the card over and placed it on the table between herself and Charlie.

The imagery was as ancient as the card itself. A tree, and beneath it, a man and a woman, in medieval costume, hands joined as they faced one another. Above, a winged creature—perhaps an angel—overlooked their union.

"The Lovers," said Mr. Deeley without hesitation.

"You know the Tarot?" Charlie asked, surprised.

"I do. And I know this card in particular. I have drawn it before."

"With this card," Esmerelda said to Charlie, "The Fool has undertaken a journey. He has arrived at a place where the single road divides. At this crossroads he beholds a tree, and a woman. The Fool has found love."

The Gypsy pointed to a place to the left of the card.

"His intention was to take this road."

She then indicated an imaginary place to the right of the card, where the woman was standing.

"But he must also now consider this road, if his love be strong. The first path is easy, but without reward. The second path promises hardship, but a bounty of love. The Fool must make his choice."

"So The Lovers is actually about a fool, some woman he met on the road, and the timelessness of love?" Charlie asked, not entirely seriously. "I think this could be a song by Bob Dylan..."

"This is the card of choice," Esmerelda replied patiently. "The choice of the head. The choice of the heart. Love always comes at a cost. But The Fool has the knowledge to make his choice wisely, and for the good of all involved. If the correct choice is made, the fire will burn long and bright. The power of love transcends all time."

"This seems to be more about you than me," Charlie said, looking at Mr. Deeley.

"More fool me," Mr. Deeley joked gently. "I understand the message, Esmerelda. Even if the woman I have met on the road does not."

"Has your question been answered?" Esmerelda inquired.

Charlie thought for a moment.

"Not really." She reached for her bag. "What do I owe you?"

"You owe me nothing," Esmerelda replied. "My payment is the completion of your journey."

— ◇ —

Charlie blinked in the bright sunlight. The Tarot reading had left her feeling slightly disoriented. Inside the tent, it had been shady and quiet. Outside, it was suddenly noisy. A punk band, comprised of Stoneford's tattooed best, was warming up on a stage near the dunk tank.

Charlie remembered why they'd originally come to the fair.

"I must introduce you to Natalie," she said to Mr. Deeley as she finished her sausage roll.

But as they walked back towards the museum's tent, Charlie was jostled. No, not jostled, pushed. Hard. So that she crashed into Mr. Deeley, who caught her in his arms and stopped her falling to the ground.

As she struggled to regain her balance, the man who had pushed her hooked his hand through the strap of her bag and yanked it off her shoulder.

"Hey!" Charlie shouted, but he was already halfway across the green.

With Mr. Deeley and Charlie chasing after him, the man looped around, then skidded into Esmerelda's tent, disappearing inside.

Charlie and Mr. Deeley followed.

"Where is he?" Charlie demanded, confronting the fortune teller. "The man who stole my bag. He ran in here. We both saw him."

Esmerelda drew a curtain of glittering beads aside.

"Go through," she suggested.

Charlie led the way, followed by Mr. Deeley, but the back of the tent was empty. There was, however, a second opening in the scarlet and lilac panels, and it led outside.

Charlie and Mr. Deeley exited the tent.

And, in doing so, immediately became aware that something was different.

Quite different, in fact.

The Village Green was still their Village Green. And the annual village fair still occupied it. But this was not twenty-first century Stoneford.

Instead of cleverly designed tents with pickles, preserves and pedicures, there were wooden stalls and temporary booths featuring acrobats and tightrope walkers. Puppet shows. Ventriloquists and waxworks. The Amazing Pig of Knowledge that could tell you what time it was. The Fireproof Lady who could thrust her arm into a fire, and warm her hands in boiling oil. A Perfect Sea Nymph. The Two-Headed Child (*She is Alive!*). The Celebrated Dutch Dwarf. A boxing competition was in progress beside the Village Oak. And the square was filled with any number of carts and barrows hawking sausages and hot pies, gingerbread and roasted nuts.

The Village Green was more crowded with fairgoers than Charlie could ever remember, even going back to the fairs of her childhood. The women wore frocks with long skirts and tiny waists, full sleeves and high necks. The men were in white shirts, waistcoats and cotton trousers. And little girls in pinafores and small boys in cloth caps chased each other through the crowd.

"Mrs. Collins," Mr. Deeley said. "I do believe we have travelled to another time. Yet again."

"I do believe you are correct, Mr. Deeley," Charlie replied.

There was a barrow directly in front of her, and its owner was selling, not roasted sausages or chestnuts, but second-hand books.

"Although this cannot be 1825, Mr. Deeley. This gentleman's wares include *Jane Eyre* and *Wuthering Heights*. Sir, can you tell me what year this is?"

The barrowman looked surprised.

"Eighteen hundred and forty-eight, madam," he replied. "May I interest you in the poems of Currer, Ellis and Acton Bell?"

"Thank you," Charlie said. "I have their first book of poetry and all of their novels at home. They're better known as the Brontë sisters. Charlotte, Emily and Anne."

"*Women?*" the barrowman laughed, with utter contempt. "God help England if we allow women to write. Next they will want a say in running the country!"

"Your current monarch is a woman," Charlie reminded him.

"There is your thief," Mr. Deeley said suddenly. "And he is still in possession of your bag. Come, follow me."

Charlie ran after her companion as he weaved quickly through the hawkers, jugglers and the shouting showmen, the strolling women and men and the laughing children.

They emerged at the top end of the green, opposite The Dog's Watch Inn. The robber had stopped running and now stood beside a wooden bench, catching his breath.

Glancing up, he saw Charlie and Mr. Deeley. And then, very deliberately, he placed Charlie's bag on the bench. And before Mr. Deeley could close the distance, he sprinted away, disappearing back into the crowd.

Charlie seized her bag.

She'd once had her purse snatched in London, and had found it lying in the gutter a block away, minus her credit card, some cash, and her phone.

But now, her wallet and money were untouched. Her phone was still tucked into the bag's zippered side pocket.

Mr. Deeley had returned, slightly out of breath and laden with apologies.

"I regret I was unable to apprehend the villain," he said, "in spite of giving chase. He is a master at his craft."

"Not that much of a master," Charlie said. "He left everything behind in my purse. And he had plenty of time to rifle through it."

She slung the bag over her shoulder.

"Let's go home, Mr. Deeley. I'd rather not be stuck in Victorian Stoneford, if it's all the same to you."

"Catherine!"

At first, Charlie paid no attention to the shouted name as she and Mr. Deeley made their way back towards the Gypsy's fortune-telling tent.

"Catherine! Wait! Wait!"

It was Mr. Deeley who at last stopped walking and drew Charlie's attention to the woman who was hurrying after them.

"Can this be your cousin?" he inquired.

It was indeed. And due to a confusion of introductions in 1825, when Charlie had first met the woman destined to become her great-grand-mother, six times into the past, Charlie would forever be known to her as Catherine Collins. A visiting cousin from London.

"Sarah!" Charlie said, taking her ancestor's hands and pulling her into a hug, quite in opposition to the manners of the day.

Sarah was twenty-three years older than the last time they had met. She was a mature woman of fifty-five now, with gracefully greying hair and a not-unbecoming figure that was somewhat plumper than Charlie remembered.

"But you have not changed in any way at all!" Sarah exclaimed. "In-deed, Catherine, you must take me in your confidence and reveal your secret of youth! And, my goodness, what a surprise this is! What brings you here?"

"I've come to see the fair, of course," Charlie replied, thinking quickly.

"And Mr. Deeley!" Sarah continued. "I am happy beyond measure to set eyes upon you once again. The last news we received was that you had been confined to the insane asylum at Bethlem Hospital in London. And wrongly so, I have always maintained. Have you managed to affect an escape?"

"He has been released, Sarah," Charlie said. "He was examined by the physician and pronounced cured. And as you can see, Mr. Deeley is in full possession of his faculties."

"It was a dreadful miscarriage of justice," Mr. Deeley supplied. "And an experience I hope never to repeat. When I think of the poor suffering souls still incarcerated within those miserable, dripping walls..."

"Mr. Deeley," Charlie said humorously, "I think you may be allowing your imagination a little too much exercise."

In fact, Mr. Deeley had been spirited away with Charlie, to her own time, before ever setting foot in Bethlem Hospital. Another confusion of identities had occurred, and someone else—someone much more deserving of the fate—had taken his place.

"And what of your husband, and your children?" Charlie asked Sarah. "Augustus and Emily."

"My dear, I regret our exchange of letters has fallen into disrepair as of late. My husband still enjoys excellent health. Emily is happily married to Mr. Pye, and has recently encouraged young Alexander to take his first steps. And as for Augustus..."

Her voice faltered.

Charlie shared a quick look of doubt with Mr. Deeley. Augustus was her direct ancestor. Without him, she would not be.

"What is it, Sarah? Has something dreadful happened?"

"He will reach the age of nineteen in a few short months," Sarah said, "yet when I consider this, I am reminded of someone so much younger. He is stubborn, Catherine, and prone to outbursts of impatient anger. He was a clever scholar, but was more taken with causing disruptions during his lessons than learning. Mr. Jenkins, the headmaster, should have caned him, but poor Augustus was of such a delicate constitution that he dared not. I often wished he had. It would have taught the boy some manners, if nothing else."

"No," Charlie said, thoughtfully, "no...it is a very good thing Mr. Jenkins did not employ his cane. It might have killed him."

"Why do you say that, dear cousin?"

Charlie paused. How to explain?

"You know of Victoria, our Queen..."

"Of course! She is very popular amongst the villagers. In fact, she has bestowed her presence upon us twice, both times making a detour while on her way to the Isle of Wight with her consort, the prince."

"She carries a gene," Charlie said. "A disease. To do with her blood."

Sarah looked horrified. "Our lovely Queen is unwell...?"

"No, no!" Charlie assured her. "She is in perfect health. But you remember, Sarah, how I once told you I was able to know about your future..."

"I do recall," Sarah said. "And everything you revealed to me has come to pass. My marriage to Louis Augustus Duran. The births of our two children, Augustus and Emily... I will never understand how you divined such knowledge, dear Catherine. But perhaps it is better I remain in ignorance."

"I'm going to tell you something about Queen Victoria's children," Charlie said. "One already born, and two yet to be. Princess Alice, who is five years old now. Another daughter, Princess Beatrice, will be born in nine years' time. And a son, Prince Leopold, will arrive five years from now. The two daughters will inherit the disease..." Charlie corrected herself. "They will inherit the condition. And they will pass it down to some of their children, though they themselves will not become ill, as it rarely affects women. Prince Leopold will also inherit the condition, but because of the way it appears in the blood, he will become ill. And he will die at a young age because of it. Before his 31st birthday."

"Oh!" Sarah said. "How terribly sad for our dear Queen!"

"But the thing is, Sarah...that same gene...that same condition of the blood...is present in our family, too. I've done the research. Look at Augustus. He bruises and bleeds too easily. And he was always a sickly child, with terrible pains in his limbs. You have observed this, haven't you?"

"I have," Sarah admitted. "And I readily confess, it has led me to be overly protective of him. Although now I see that my good intentions have led him to be spoiled, as he is prone to petulance and distemper."

Their conversation was interrupted by a commotion coming from the middle of the fair, in front of the booth which featured The Amazing Pig of Knowledge.

"Oh no," Sarah said. "A familiar voice."

She rushed off, followed by Charlie and Mr. Deeley.

The voice did indeed belong to Sarah's eighteen-year-old son, Augustus. Charlie was struck by the similarity between this youth and her own father, Justin, who might have been his twin, at almost the same age, in the mid-1960s. Two men separated by five generations, sharing a mop of unruly hair, a look of utter impertinence, accepting nothing as given, questioning all.

Charlie liked him immediately.

"This, sir," said Augustus, holding a roasted sausage aloft on a stick, "is the foulest article I have ever had the misfortune to encounter. It is not fit for human consumption. I venture it is not even pork, but some hitherto unknown substance, possibly not even animal in origin."

"You owe me sixpence, sir!" the sausage-seller replied indignantly. "And another sixpence, for the previous sausage you consumed."

"Highway robbery!" Augustus pronounced. "I shall pay you nothing, sir, as the first sausage was procured in order that I might assess its gastronomical qualities. And having thus determined its lack of same, this second sausage shall serve as a warning to all present who might be tricked into believing it edible."

"One shilling, sir!" the sausage-seller persisted, "or I shall have you arrested for theft!"

"Oh dear," said Augustus, feigning alarm. "The Stoneford Constabulary. Report me, then. In my defense I shall accuse you of fraud. This is not a pleasant sausage. It is, in fact, quite offal!"

He laughed outrageously at his joke, and was joined by several other youths.

"Tell him off properly, Augustus!" one of them shouted. "Make him eat his words!" He threw a sausage of his own at the seller, to even more laughter.

A second youth picked up the sausage, which had fallen onto the grass, and spat on it. "Hogwash!" he announced, much to the amusement of the others.

"Has there been an infraction here? A misdemeanour wanting correction?"

With a sinking feeling Charlie recognized Lemuel Ferryman, proprietor of The Dog's Watch Inn. When she had first encountered him in 1825, he'd been the village's magistrate. Surely that had changed now. New laws had since been enacted concerning crime and punishment and enforcement. Surely, by 1848, Stoneford had a proper police force.

"Shall I arrest him, Mr. Ferryman?"

It was Obediah Reader, Lemuel Ferryman's right-hand man, who did double-duty as the village constable.

"Nothing has changed here," Mr. Deeley said quietly to Charlie.

Boldly, he stepped forward.

"Mr. Ferryman, there is no need for an arrest. This young gentleman, distracted by the temptation of a fine pork sausage, has merely forgotten to pay for it. There must be a shilling in your pocket, Mr. Duran. Come and compensate the seller, and let that be an end to it."

"I shall not, sir," Augustus replied. "The sausages were reprehensible and not worth tuppence, let alone twelvepence. You should arrest the barrowman, Mr. Reader, for falsely claiming his wares to be edible."

With that he poked his stick into a third sausage and, reclaiming it from the hot coals, hurled it some distance over the heads of the gathered spectators. It struck the wall of the wooden booth housing The Amazing Pig of Knowledge and bounced unceremoniously to the ground.

Exasperated, Mr. Deeley dug into his own pockets and withdrew some change.

"There," he said, placing the money in the barrowman's hand.

"What counterfeit is this?" the sausage-seller demanded, scrutinizing the three 5p coins. "More villainy! These coins are worthless!"

"New money," Charlie said hopelessly to Mr. Deeley. "It was all switched in 1971. Decimalization."

"I know you, sir," said Lemuel Ferryman, staring at Mr. Deeley's face. "Mr. Reader, is this not the arsonist who set fire to my inn, who was declared insane and deported shortly thereafter to the asylum in London?"

"Falsely accused," Mr. Deeley corrected, before Charlie could stop him. "And falsely sentenced. And now happily released, no thanks to you."

"It is the very same," Obediah Reader confirmed. "Shaun Deeley. The groom employed at the manor."

"Released you may be," said Lemuel Ferryman. "But your new-found freedom does you no favours if you are now keeping company with this delinquent."

"For pity's sake," Sarah said, taking her son by the arm. "Pay the man his due and let us leave this place."

"I have no money, mother," Augustus replied simply, turning out his pockets. "As you can see."

"Then I shall pay!" Sarah decided. "If you will allow me the time needed to return home and collect the required sum."

"But a crime has been committed," Lemuel Ferryman said. "This cannot be allowed to stand."

"She's offered to go and get the man his money," Charlie said. "What difference can it possibly make?"

"What difference?" Ferryman roared, becoming very red in the face. "The difference is principle, madam. The difference is honesty and intent. This boy has readily admitted he has no money. He never had any money. Therefore his intent is clear. He intended to remove the sausages from this vendor's cart without any inclination towards paying.

Furthermore, he is unrepentant. Seize him, Mr. Reader. We shall teach him a lesson at the whipping post."

"No!" Charlie shouted, horrified. "Please! This cannot happen!"

"My son's constitution is delicate," Sarah pleaded. "I beg you to reconsider, and release him to my care."

"It is your featherbed coddling, madam, which is now largely responsible for this young man's reprehensible behaviour. He should have been whipped at school, regularly and soundly. He would have learned the value of honesty and the perils of impertinence. Take him away, Mr. Reader."

The gathered crowd followed as Obediah Reader dragged Augustus by the arm, away from the sausage cart, towards the top end of the Village Green.

"Sir!" the young man protested loudly. "You are hurting me, sir!"

"He shall shortly hurt you a good deal more," Ferryman promised.

"Did I understand you correctly?" Mr. Deeley asked as he followed along with Charlie. "He suffers from an illness which causes him to bleed too easily if injured?"

"It could cause him to bleed to death," Charlie answered. "It's in my family. Passed down from generation to generation. The most serious variant there is. It all apparently originated with Sarah, who passed it on to Augustus. Who will marry Edwina Sewell in 1850, and have four children, two sons and two daughters. One of the daughters and one of the sons will carry the condition in their blood. And Augustus himself will die from it at the age of 34."

"Well," said Mr. Deeley, with perfect logic, "if he marries in 1850, and lives until middle age, then he obviously will not bleed to death this afternoon."

"Mr. Deeley," Charlie said, "we have accidentally travelled back to 1848. I made a similar journey last month, to your time. I faced a moral dilemma over whether or not to interfere with history. If I had not, for instance, ensured that Sarah attended the Grand Summer Ball at the manor, and a picnic the following day, then almost certainly she would never have met her husband, thus ensuring the birth of Augustus, and so on down the line, to me."

"But if you had not made the journey," Mr. Deeley reasoned, "perhaps Sarah would have met her husband in any case. It would simply have been by other means."

"Then think about this. If I had not made the journey, I would not have met you. And you would not have come with me to my time. And you would also not now be here, with me, in 1848. I believe there could be many alternate realities, Mr. Deeley. And what we do, or don't do, while inhabiting these realities, directly affects the outcome of our future realities. Something must happen to stop this whipping. Something must *have* happened. Or I would not be here, now, talking to you."

She glanced worriedly at the top end of the green, where the crowd was now assembling, with rather more anticipation than she would have liked, in front of the whipping post.

"Much as I fear for the health of poor Augustus," said Mr. Deeley, "we know he *will* marry in two years' time, and father four children. You are proof of that. I propose, Mrs. Collins, that we consult someone who claims to know the future much better than we do."

———◆———

Esmerelda was still sitting at her cloth-covered table, with her deck of Tarot cards.

"Have you found the answer to your question?" she inquired.

"No," Charlie replied. "And now we are faced with a dilemma. To interfere..."

"Or not," said Mr. Deeley.

"Your journey is not finished."

Charlie glared at the Gypsy.

"You," she said, "are not being helpful. At all."

Esmerelda shuffled the Tarot deck and offered it to Charlie. "Choose."

"No. I've played that game. For all I know, your cards are all the same."

Esmerelda said nothing. She turned the deck of cards over on the table, and fanned them out. All were distinctly different, a full suit of Tarot.

She gathered the cards back into a single stack again, and this time offered it to Mr. Deeley.

"Choose," she said.

Mr. Deeley selected a single card from the middle of the deck, and, without looking at it, gave it to the Gypsy.

Esmerelda held the card up.

"It is The Lovers," Mr. Deeley said simply. "Again."

"It is the card of choice," Esmerelda corrected. "The Fool at the crossroads. Remember when last we met, *gorgio*. You chose your path wisely then. Choose it again now."

The whipping post was very old, an upright timber that had been erected two hundred years earlier. However, in the 19th century, it had fallen into disuse as law and order became standardized throughout the country.

There were, however, the holdouts. And it appeared that Stoneford was one of those villages.

The law, as dictated by Lemuel Ferryman, still prevailed.

Augustus Duran, accused, found guilty and sent down for punishment in a matter of moments, stood with his shirt removed and his hands fastened to the post, his face still bearing an expression of complete defiance.

Nearby was Sarah, as pale as a ghost.

And beside her the village physician, Dr. Owen, was consulting with Lemuel Ferryman and Obediah Reader.

"The young man's constitution is frail," he concluded, "but not so frail as to disallow an example to be made of his decidedly un-frail behaviour. Perhaps the aftermath will serve to teach a lesson in civility. You may proceed."

"Mr. Ferryman," Charlie said, stepping forward. "Is there really no way to mitigate the damages and avoid this punishment? His mother has already offered to pay for the sausages. Can you not place this young man in custody instead, and have him serve a sentence in the lockup in your cellar? A week? Two weeks?"

"You again," said Lemuel Ferryman impatiently.

"A custodial sentence has been imposed upon several previous occasions," Obediah Reader provided. "And it seems to have had little effect on the young man's distemper."

"He will die if you beat him," Charlie said.

"I doubt that," Dr. Owen answered.

"Sir, I implore you. You have studied medicine. You must know of the condition which causes a person to bleed without cessation. I'm sure it has been written about in your medical journals. Augustus Duran suffers from that same condition. I know this to be true."

Dr. Owen looked unsure.

"A dozen strokes, and one for good measure," Lemuel Ferryman decided, "and let that be an end to it. The boy has broken two of my windows with deliberately aimed rocks. He and his friends hurl insults at me whenever they pass me in the street. He chalks rude words upon brick walls and causes his mother immeasurable grief. And now he has resorted to thievery. These are the makings of a life of delinquency. Lay on, Mr. Reader."

"Wait," said Mr. Deeley as Obediah Reader stepped forward with a nasty-looking implement made up of nine leather straps fastened to a short handle. "It was I who stole the sausages."

Lemuel Ferryman laughed.

"It was not you who stole the sausages, sir. It was this young man. There are witnesses."

"The witnesses are mistaken," said Mr. Deeley. "It was me."

"What are you saying, Mr. Deeley?" Charlie whispered. "You had nothing to do with this!"

"Clearly," said Mr. Deeley, "Mr. Ferryman is of a mind to make an example of this youth. From my own experience, I believe it will have little overall effect on his attitude, other than to make him even more rebellious and encourage him to commit even more serious crimes."

"What is your proposal, sir?" Lemuel Ferryman asked.

"I will take his punishment."

Charlie was speechless.

"Mrs. Collins," Mr. Deeley said quietly. "I believe that my road of choice has led to this. Otherwise there is no point to our presence. Your bag was deliberately taken in order to bring us here. I fear we will be unable to return to our own time unless we interfere."

Charlie could see that Augustus, who had been watching and listening from the whipping post, was as incredulous as she was. In fact, she thought, he looked almost annoyed.

"There, you see a fool at the crossroads."

"I see a fool beside me," Charlie replied unhappily.

"We both selected the card of choice," Mr. Deeley reminded her. "And this is mine."

He stepped forward, undoing the buttons of his shirt.

"Release the youth," he said to Lemuel Ferryman, "and fasten me to the post instead. Do you agree?"

"This is highly irregular."

"Come, sir. You harbour no kind feelings towards me. You were convinced I tried to burn down your inn, and were never happier than when you proclaimed I should hang for the crime. That my sentence was commuted to confinement at Bethlem Hospital must have left you with untold frustration. And Mr. Reader was very liberal with his fists, and a boot, when charged with arresting me. The arson occurred in the middle of the night and he was roused from a comfortable bed in order to see justice done. The only thing stopping him from inflicting further damage to my person was his need for sleep."

Mr. Deeley took off his shirt, which, Charlie noted, elicited a faintly perceptible sigh from some of the women who had gathered in the front row to witness the punishment.

"It will not kill me," he assured her. "Unlike your ancestor."

"At least you'll have an appreciative audience," Charlie replied.

Mr. Deeley turned to Lemuel Ferryman.

"One further request. That Augustus Duran be required to stand beside me, to act as my witness."

Ferryman relayed the request to the miscreant as Obediah Reader loosed his wrists from the iron ring where they'd been tied.

"I would rather not," Augustus replied.

"All the more reason to insist that you do," Ferryman said. "You will stand there, sir."

This, Augustus did, with very bad grace, as Mr. Deeley took his place at the whipping post.

"Now then," Mr. Deeley said, as his hands were tied fast to the iron ring with a length of rope. "Listen to me, and listen well, as this is a lesson I offer you, in private. It will be worth more to you than the whole of the education you have received from your long-suffering headmaster, Mr. Jenkins."

"I do not know you, sir," Augustus replied. "But I will tell you, I consider you a fool."

"You are not the first to come to that conclusion." He stopped, because Obediah Reader had delivered the first blow, and it had not been a gentle one. "And I daresay you will not be the last. I am guaranteeing you a future, Mr. Duran. And in so doing, I am guaranteeing the future of the woman I hold dearest to my heart."

The second blow was not as harsh as the first, although that might have been his imagination. Mr. Deeley did not expect Obediah Reader to do him any favours.

A young woman in the front row of spectators was beginning to weep.

Mr. Deeley glanced at Charlie, who shook her head, still unwilling to accept what she was witnessing.

The third blow was as excruciating as the first.

"Mr. Duran," he continued. "Oblige me with your attention, as my own may be very shortly distracted. You have an illness. It does not seem to have rendered you an invalid, but your physical constitution is not strong. I am not incorrect."

"You are not," Augustus admitted.

The fourth blow from the whip caused Mr. Deeley to swear. He glanced again at Charlie, hoping she hadn't heard.

She looked at him. There were tears in her eyes.

"This condition has caused you to suffer, but your suffering has, in turn, caused others to grant you concessions. Where stronger individuals might have been taken to task, you were excused. You have used this excuse to your advantage, Mr. Duran. As you have taken advantage of those who care most for your wellbeing."

He stopped, as the fifth blow knocked the wind out of him. He grasped the stout ropes that immobilized his hands in the iron ring.

Eight yet to come.

"Are you not concerned," he said, "that your behaviour causes your mother such upset?"

"Ought I to be concerned?"

"That is a selfish attitude, sir." He paused. "What was your purpose in stealing the sausages?"

"I wished to make an example of the rogue. His wares are foul. The meat comes from the basest scraps on the slaughterhouse floor. I have seen this with my own eyes. My friend John is the son of the butcher."

The sixth blow of the whip was as unforgiving as the first, and Mr. Deeley was aware that the stinging cuts were beginning to bleed.

Obediah Reader took a moment to rest his arm.

"Your principles are admirable," Mr. Deeley said, "if somewhat misdirected...I will tell you something about your mother. She refused to marry a man she did not love. Even though she was faced with financial ruin and a future defined by poverty. She remained faithful to her principles. And, in time, she was introduced to your father, without whom you would not be."

"I had not heard this," Augustus said. "How do you come by this knowledge?"

"I know a good deal about the past, before you were born," Mr. Deeley advised. "And I know a good deal about your future, as well. Miss Edwina Sewell. You are acquainted with her?"

"I am. In fact, she is behind you. She weeps for your suffering."

"And you harbour an affection for this lady?...Bloody hell."

This last was in reaction to the seventh blow. His ordeal was now more than half finished, and Mr. Deeley could hear Miss Sewell's loud sobs nearby. He lowered his head, so that his forehead was pressed against the wooden post.

The eighth blow landed on his shoulders, and Mr. Deeley closed his eyes.

"Mr. Duran," he repeated. "Do you harbour an affection for Miss Sewell?"

"I do," Augustus admitted. "However, she holds me in contempt, and I cannot imagine any sort of agreement to marriage. Her parents in particular would rather I transfer my affections elsewhere."

"I cannot argue with their wisdom," Mr. Deeley said haltingly, as the ninth blow cut across the welts left by the other eight. "But hear me...within the next two years...you will marry Miss Sewell...and you will have four children...whose names...unfortunately...escape me..."

The tenth blow caused him to gasp.

"How can you be certain of this?" Augustus asked. There was less pomposity in his voice, and his self-assured haughtiness had all but disappeared.

"You will have to accept my word," Mr. Deeley said. "I assure you...this will all come to pass...but only if you have the will...to alter your direction...and cease this wasting of your life. Otherwise...I fear you will end up in prison...or dead."

Eleven.

"There is still time to change your ways."

"Why are you telling me these things?" Augustus asked, his voice now clearly troubled. "And why have you endured the punishment that should have come to me?"

Twelve.

"I have already told you that my motives...are entirely selfish... If I had not...this beating would almost certainly...have killed you. Thus depriving me..."

Thirteen.

"Release the prisoner's hands, Mr. Reader."

"...of the love of my life."

"I do not pretend to understand your logic, sir," Augustus said slowly. "But I cannot agree that your motives are selfish. I can see with my own eyes the damage that has been inflicted upon you. I believe that you have performed an act of utmost generosity. For if this damage had been inflicted upon me, I know that, with certainty, I would not recover."

Mr. Deeley hugged the wooden post as the feeling came back into his hands, and he struggled to recover his sense of balance. His back was on fire.

Behind him, Miss Sewell had fainted, and was being brought to her senses by a stout lady in black with a vial of smelling salts and a good deal of handkerchief waving.

Charlie was at Mr. Deeley's side.

"Will you agree to consider what I have suggested to you?" he said to Augustus. "I ask only that. I trust you will make the right decision, and choose your road wisely."

"I shall consider it, sir. You have my word. For now, I am intrigued as much about your knowledge of my mother's past, and your predictions for my own future, as I am about your reasons for accepting my punishment. When you have sufficiently recovered, may we revisit this conversation?"

Mr. Deeley smiled.

"Go and comfort poor Miss Sewell," he suggested. "And ask her what names she favours for two sons and two daughters."

———◆○◆———

"Albert, Louise, Victoria and Alfred," Charlie said, as they walked back towards the Gypsy's tent. "What else were you two talking about?"

"I was merely attempting to convince your ancestor to change his foolish ways."

"Merely," Charlie said, shaking her head. "And were you successful?"

"I think so," said Mr. Deeley. "Time will tell, I suppose."

He laughed at his joke, then stopped abruptly, because of the pain it was causing him.

"And do you have experience in the foolish ways of youth?" Charlie inquired.

"I do, in fact. It was an individual, not unlike my adult self, who took me aside at much the same age as young Augustus, and delivered a lecture which set me on a far more promising path than the one I had been following."

"Interesting," Charlie said. "And did you know this individual, or was he some random stranger that happened to bump into you at the annual village fair?"

"He was a random stranger," Mr. Deeley replied, surprising her. "And it was, in fact, at the village fair."

"Fascinating," Charlie said. "Did this random stranger happen to predict that you would meet me?"

"He did."

"Really?"

Mr. Deeley smiled.

"Did you ever learn his name?"

"I did not. Although, in retrospect, I believe he may have borne a passing resemblance to the thief who took your bag."

"I can't ever imagine you stealing sausages," Charlie said with a laugh, holding the tent flap open for her companion.

"It was not sausages," Mr. Deeley replied. "But it was the same whipping post."

———◦———

Esmerelda was waiting for them at her cloth-covered table.

"Your journey is almost finished."

"There is more?" Mr. Deeley asked faintly, steadying himself on one of the chairs on the table's opposite side.

"If the correct choice is made," Esmerelda repeated, "the fire will burn long and bright. Has your question been answered?"

"I believe it has," Charlie said, taking Mr. Deeley's hand. "I cannot imagine a braver soul than this gentleman, nor a more caring one."

"You cause me to blush, Mrs. Collins."

"You are, in fact, my hero."

She kissed him, which caused him to blush even more. There were, she thought, some rather nice mannerisms attached to someone who had been born in 1791.

Esmerelda placed a small glass vial on the table.

"Take this unguent and apply it to his back. The recipe is an old one, passed down through the generations in my family. He will heal quickly, and without complication."

"You knew all this was going to happen, didn't you?" Charlie said, putting the vial into her bag.

"Be on your way," the Gypsy replied. "*Baxt hai sastimos tiri patragi*. Until our paths may cross again."

———◦———

Outside the tent, the punk rock band on the stage beside the dunk tank had launched into something thoroughly discordant and full of anger.

"This noise assaults my ears," Mr. Deeley judged. "Take me home, Mrs. Collins. I am in need of your tender care, the gypsy's ointment, and my bed."

They walked together across the Village Green.

"I am curious," said Mr. Deeley. "How did Augustus earn his living, after he married Miss Sewell and fathered his four children?"

"He practised law, Mr. Deeley. And became a noted defender of the downtrodden and disadvantaged. Hundreds of people mourned his passing when he died from complications resulting from a fall."

"Ah," said Mr. Deeley.

"I don't believe any of that would have happened, but for you."

Mr. Deeley considered the sky, and then smiled, once again, and with a good deal of satisfaction.

At the edge of the green, Charlie looked back. She could see the spot where Esmerelda's tent stood.

Or had stood.

It seemed not to be there anymore.

In its place was an open square of grass, which was occupied by a street magician. He wore a white top hat and a white silk cape, which, in the fading daylight, seemed to take on the characteristics of a pair of long, folded wings.

A magician who looked, Charlie thought, as she and Mr. Deeley crossed the road that led to her cottage, uncannily like the fellow who had stolen her bag. Or, perhaps, an angel.

ABOUT PERHAPS AN ANGEL..

In 2013, Fable Press published my first accidental time travel romance, *Persistence of Memory*.

To help publicise our books, a group of Fable Press authors (including me) got together that same year to write and publish an anthology of short stories centered around the theme of "Carnival".

The result was an eBook, also called *Carnival*, which is, unfortunately, no longer available. My story, "Perhaps an Angel", was an adventure involving my two main characters from *Persistence of Memory*, contemporary time traveller Charlie Duran and her companion from 1825, Shaun Deeley.

The story takes place chronologically between *Persistence of Memory* and the next book in the series, *In Loving Memory*.

8

EASY WHEN YOU KNOW HOW

"It is mornings like this," Mr. Deeley said softly, "which I longed for. The rareness of being able to lie in my bed, listening to the birds, who have been awake since before sunrise, chattering to each other, exchanging gossip and scandalous stories concerning families in the next village."

Charlie laughed. She snuggled closer to Mr. Deeley, into the hollow between his armpit and his chest, resting her head on his arm as his hand cradled her shoulder, drawing her close.

"Did you not have any chance at all for a lie-in?" she inquired.

"Never. The horses needed to be cared for, and although there were stable boys, they were notoriously unreliable. For this I blame the lesser Monsieur Duran, as he had a hand in their hiring, and would never allow me to make sensible decisions. In any case, the servants of the manor were expected to rise at the appointed hour. And as I was not keen to be dismissed, I embraced the expectations."

"Well," Charlie said. "You're in my world now, and in my world, you're allowed to lie in bed for as long as you want. Provided, of course, that we put in an appearance at the museum before lunchtime. Expectations, and all that."

Mr. Deeley smiled, turned a little, and kissed her. It was a gentle kiss, a good morning kiss, for although they, like the sparrows in the apple trees outside her bedroom window, had been awake for hours, they had not been sleeping. And so it was a kiss that reaffirmed the goodness of everything that had gone on that morning, and the night before, and every day and night before that, since the moment they'd first met on the Village Green.

She was wearing a nightgown that he had bought her. She had no idea where he'd found it. It was very old, and very simple...a fine white cotton, almost see-through but not quite...the old-fashioned term for it was *batiste*. It had a plunging neckline and short sleeves, and it was trimmed at the bottom with beautiful Ile d'Aix lace—she'd looked it up.

He had presented it to her one afternoon, after he'd mysteriously disappeared for two hours, without any sort of explanation.

"It is French," he had said simply. "Worn by the Empress Josephine herself."

Charlie had laughed. "That would make it an absolute antique, Mr. Deeley. And incredibly valuable. What did you do—slip into Napoleon's chateau yourself and steal it from her wardrobe?"

She'd meant it as a joke, but in retrospect, Charlie wondered if she had guessed at the truth—or something very close to it.

Mr. Deeley, like herself, was a time traveller—more accidental than by design. But, unlike her, he had been practicing. She was hesitant to experiment; Mr. Deeley was filled with the sense of adventure, and had no qualms about trying out his fledgling wings...much to Charlie's consternation.

"What would happen if you weren't able to come back?" she'd asked. "What would happen if you got stuck in whatever time you landed in? At least let me know when you're going to go flying off to whenever...so Nick and I can launch a search party for you if you don't come back!"

Mr. Deeley had laughed it off, but Charlie couldn't dismiss his random adventures so easily.

"We really should get moving," she said, kissing the special place on his bare chest that tickled him and made him laugh in the most delighted and wonderful way.

"I shall make breakfast," he decided. "Is what we eat for breakfast now the same as what they ate for breakfast in the time of your new display?"

"Somewhat the same," Charlie said. She slid out of bed and watched as he climbed out of bed too, fully naked but still a little bit shy about showing her his body, even after so many months of sharing her bed. Old attitudes from 1825 were very hard to break. "But in the Swinging Sixties they were still going to work on a boiled egg...they didn't have the variety of food that we have now. And especially not Honey Nut Crunch with Milk Chocolate Curls."

"My favourite," Mr. Deeley said, looking at her as she slipped out of her nightgown and, she knew, very much admiring what he saw. "Why was it called the Swinging Sixties, Mrs. Collins? Was there some sort of...suspension involved?"

"Suspension of old attitudes and beliefs, perhaps, Mr. Deeley," Charlie said. "It was a time of incredible change in England. All the children who were born during the war, or just after it, had grown up and were looking for something new, something different. My mum was just the right age. She worked in a boutique. She kept a lot of her clothes from that time. She's sending me a genuine Mary Quant mini-dress. And I've got some of her other things...some old magazines and newspapers, and a lot of her vinyl records. Albums and 45s."

Mr. Deeley was pretending to understand, but Charlie was certain he had no idea at all what she was talking about. The Swinging Sixties display at the Stoneford Village Museum was still only in the planning stages.

Her mobile rang.

"Leave it," Mr. Deeley suggested, giving her another kiss. "I am impatient for my Honey Nut Crunch."

"I must answer it," Charlie said. "It's Giles Jessop."

———◇———

"And who is Giles Jessop?" Mr. Deeley inquired. He had put on a pair of very worn jeans, and an Italian cotton knit jumper, and he was barefoot. Charlie thought he looked amazingly sexy as he poured milk into their cereal bowls, and tea into two mugs.

"A very famous singer from the 1960s," she said. "He was born in Stoneford and was part of the British Invasion of America. He had a band. Brighton Peer."

"Named after the very famous pier?"

"No, though it's a play on that. His dad was an earl who was originally from Brighton. So, you know...a peer. Of the realm."

"Why did he ring you?"

"Because he's heard about my exhibit and he'd like to help out," Charlie said. "I'm quite chuffed, really. He's asked us to come to London to see him."

Charlie studied Mr. Deeley's boots. They were a lovely light brown, scuffed and creased and generally well worn-in. They were cut low so that they ended just above his ankles, but the foot was close enough in design to the sort of boots he had worn in 1825 that he felt at home in them. And they went perfectly with his jeans. And his white cotton shirt. And his tailored summer jacket. And his long, somewhat untidy, hair. He was, indeed, a man of many ages.

They were on the tube, riding from Waterloo to Piccadilly Circus, a short journey but faster than walking—their train from Middlehurst had been delayed, and they were late for their appointment with Giles Jessop.

It was Wednesday, and on Wednesdays Mr. Deeley was not required at the museum, where, three times a week, he provided horse-drawn cart rides around historical Stoneford for the tourists.

It was almost a year to the day since he'd arrived from 1825 and become such an integral part of Charlie's life that she was no longer able to imagine it without him. She remembered his first ride on the Underground—how terrified he'd been. But he'd acclimatized himself quickly after that. He had mastered the cooker in her kitchen—and she no longer lived in fear that he would try to use the fireplace to boil water for tea. He had appropriated her iPad and completely embraced the Internet, employing it to research his ancestors and his descendants, as well as hers; to buy clothes; to listen to music; to watch videos; and even, she suspected, to dip his toes into the curious world of social networking. She wondered if he had a Facebook account, and made up her mind to ask him when the subject next came up.

They surfaced at Piccadilly Circus, then walked up behind the old London Pavilion, once a music hall, then a cinema, now completely gutted inside and made into a shopping centre. Their route took them, in a few minutes, to Great Windmill Street, and Giles Jessop's £4-million flat, accessed by way of a completely unobtrusive door beside an Indonesian restaurant.

"Very apropos," Charlie said, as they walked up the stairs. "He's right round the corner from Ham Yard, which is where the Scene Club was."

"And the Scene Club was...?" Mr. Deeley inquired.

"Well known in the early 1960s for its mod subculture. The Rolling Stones used to play there. And The Who."

"Who are The Who?"

"Look them up," Charlie suggested, amused. "Roger Daltrey. *Tommy*. There's a posh hotel around there now."

Giles Jessop was 73 years old. He had a white shock of hair which had once been bright red, and a cheeky look on his face which was the same as it had been in 1964, when Brighton Peer was climbing the pop charts with songs about unrequited love and the heartache of summer goodbyes.

His flat was equally cheeky—a guest bedroom on the first floor, a kitchen and sitting room on the second, an immense master bedroom and ensuite bath on the third floor, and the entire fourth floor comprised of an open air terrace planted with exotic palms and giant plants that would have been at home in any convenient jungle. The flat itself had bare brick walls that showed off the age of the narrow little building that housed it, an abundance of black and white furniture, and maple wood accents.

"I was 23 in 1964," Giles said as they sat in comfortable canvas chairs on the open terrace. "Barely out of nappies. 'Course, we thought we knew it all. More than our parents, at any rate. We were kids in the war, which was one big bloody adventure, truth be known. Bits of hot shrapnel in the road after a raid and barrage balloons up in the sky. Our parents were so worn out and so old-fashioned. We grew up in the '50s and by the time the '60s came round we were ready to break all the rules and rewrite everything to suit ourselves. Which is what we did, of course. Have another slice of Battenberg. And some sausage rolls. More tea?"

"Yes please," Charlie said.

"And then, of course, there was Marianne."

"Marianne Faithfull?"

"A wonderful friend. But another. Marianne Dutton. We very nearly married. She had a boutique. In Carnaby Street. Full of all sorts of rubbish and old tat."

"Of course," Charlie said. "Marianne's Memory. My mum worked there. Jackie Lewis. She's about the same age as you."

"Jackie Lewis. Lovely girl. Whatever happened to her?"

"She married my dad—Justin Duran."

"Ah, yes," Giles said, "I was at school with Justin. Of course. How could I forget?"

"It was the 1960s," Mr. Deeley said humorously. "What is the famous quotation? If you remember it, you weren't there?"

"Truer words were never spoken," Giles replied. He paused, and then looked very keenly at Charlie.

"You have an older sibling."

"Yes. Two of them. Abigail. She was born in 1975. And an older brother, too. Simon. 1971."

"No darling, before them. Before your mum and dad were ever married. She had a child." Giles leaned forward, conspiratorially, and whispered: "Out of wedlock. 1964-ish. 1965."

Charlie stared at him, shocked into silence. Mr. Deeley was staring too.

"Admired her for going through with it. Things were very dodgy back then if you wanted to terminate. But she couldn't keep the child. Wouldn't. Said it would be for the best if she gave it up for adoption."

"Did my grandmother know?" Charlie asked, still stunned.

"'Course she did, darling. Jackie was sharing a flat with Marianne, but she was round her mum's all the time for tea. How could she not have known?"

"Who is the father of this child?" Mr. Deeley inquired.

"Don't know. Never did know. Don't think she ever said."

"Didn't she have a regular boyfriend that she was seeing?"

"Not then," said Giles.

"Most interesting," said Mr. Deeley.

"Yes, we all thought so too. Well. We've had a lovely lunch, and I promise if you come back next week I'll have a compendium of things for your museum display. I'll ask my mates—the ones that are still alive, at any rate—for some donations as well. Hang on and I'll give you something for the road."

He got up stiffly, favouring an arthritic hip, and collected a tiny silver box from a table just inside the door to the terrace. He opened the lid and presented it to Charlie.

"There you are."

"A plectrum," Charlie said.

"Imitation tortoiseshell. From 1964. I nicked it from John Lennon. I reckon it's worth a few thousand quid. Saw one just like it for sale at Christie's a few years back. This one doesn't have Lennon's initials on it but I can swear to its authenticity."

"Thank you," Charlie said, holding the little silver box in the palm of her hand. "If you're sure..."

"'Course I'm sure. I've had it for decades...could never think of what to do with it. Now I know. Keep it safe, darling. Put it on display and don't let on who it used to belong to. Our secret. Will you take some Battenberg with you for your journey...?"

"Where is this Carnaby Street located?" Mr. Deeley asked as they stood outside the Indonesian restaurant, attempting to get their bearings again.

"A bit further north, I think," Charlie said, consulting the map on her phone. "Yes, there. Closer to Regent Street. Would you like to see it?"

"I would," Mr. Deeley replied. "Would it look much the same after the passage of fifty years?"

"I'm not sure, Mr. Deeley. I imagine the buildings are still the same, but I think most of the original shops and boutiques are long gone. They've done it up for the tourists now. The Swinging Sixties really only happened over a couple of years. It's the idea that's survived. The music and the films and the fashion."

They negotiated the narrow back streets of Soho, traversing the history of Brewer Street and Bridle Lane, and Beak Street.

"You're very quiet, Mrs. Collins."

"I'm still in shock, Mr. Deeley. To be told that you have a brother or a sister you didn't know about...and my mum's never said anything to any of us. And my Nana—she knew about it too. Nothing."

"Perhaps it was not something that could be spoken about. Perhaps to spare the feelings of your father. And of you, and your other sister and brother."

"Back then it wasn't spoken about, you're right. But after all this time... I wonder if he or she's been trying to find us."

They had reached the bottom end of Carnaby Street, which had been blocked off to traffic.

"It seems very..." Mr. Deeley paused as he watched the tourists walking along the red brick paving stones, phones, and cameras in hand.

"Ordinary?" Charlie guessed.

"Yes. Ordinary. A very apt description." He looked up. "But for this archway welcoming us to Carnaby Street, I might be forgiven for mistaking this for any other shopping precinct in England."

"Perhaps it's a bit more...exciting... at the other end."

And so they walked, with the tourists, to the upper stretch of the famous street, and the other curved welcome sign.

"It is still very ordinary," Mr. Deeley judged, obviously disappointed. "I see nothing which convinces me this was once the hotbed of unbridled sixties swinging."

Charlie laughed. "I do love you, Mr. Deeley," she said. "Try to imagine these little shopfronts fifty years ago. There was a road running down the middle, with lots of cars. And a narrow pavement on both sides. All the women wore little Mary Quant mini-dresses, with Vidal Sassoon hair and Twiggy eyes. All the men had long hair and tight trousers and the latest jackets and boots from John Stephen." She assessed her companion. "A bit like what you're wearing now, in fact."

"Perhaps you should install me in your museum display," Mr. Deeley replied humorously. "Where is it that your mother worked?"

"I'm not entirely sure about the address. I know it was up this end...mum once showed me a picture of it."

She paused in front of a tiny shopfront painted bright blue, with wide display windows on either side of a narrow little doorway. Above the windows and door was a wide lintel, out of which was growing a mass of greenery. And above the greenery rose three floors of dwellings, two windows per floor, all of the brickwork painted a pale grey and the window frames white. The sign above the doorway, and below the greenery, read: Easy When You Know How.

"I think that might be it," Charlie said. "Change of name...and I'm not entirely sure what they're selling these days...but yes. There. Shall we go inside?"

The interior of the shop smelled of patchouli and ylang-ylang, and there was a glass wind chime hanging near the door, which tinkled with the passing breeze. Just inside the door was a table covered with spectacles: wire-framed grannies; huge plastic glasses, of the sort Deirdre Barlow wore when she first arrived in *Coronation Street*; monocles and diamante cats-eyes; and all different colours of lenses.

Spreading aspidistras and huge ferns stood on shelves and plinths, and hanging underneath those were neckties, scarves, and shawls from every age known to fashion.

Against one wall hung women's clothing, salvaged from time and second-hand shops: Victoriana, and flapper, and wide 1950s skirts that demanded crinolines and white ankle socks, and mod mini's and cotton shifts from the 1960s. Against another wall, gentlemen's apparel: military uniforms and velvet trousers, and silk shirts and flare-legged denim jeans. Dickensian coats. Leather flying jackets with sheepskin collars. Floral prints and exquisite double-breasted tailoring.

A giant silk umbrella, fully open; a two-wheeled bicycle; and cooking pots, overflowing with silk flowers were suspended from the ceiling.

There was a large sofa against the back wall, and a very ornate mirror, and a single dressing room separated from the main shop by a row of hanging glass beads.

And there was music, which seemed to be emanating from a vintage jukebox beside the mirror. Charlie recognized the song immediately.

"*House of the Rising Sun*," she said to Mr. Deeley. "The Animals. 1964."

"What a noise."

"It's a classic, Mr. Deeley!"

"Might I be of assistance?"

A woman had appeared from a room at the back. She seemed to be in her forties, or perhaps her fifties. She had long blonde hair with a full fringe and she wore a mauve frock, which might have come originally from a turn-of-the-century brothel.

"We're just looking around," Charlie said. "My mum used to work here. In the 1960s. When it was called—"

"Marianne's Memory," the woman finished. "Yes. I know. It was famous! It all rather fell into hard times after the 1960s though... it sat empty for ages...and then it was a poster shop...and then a touristy souvenir sort of place, maps and flags and t-shirts and mugs...A shoe store. A place that sold mobile phones. And then it was empty again...I've tried to make it as much like the original as possible."

"Why Easy When You Know How?" Mr. Deeley inquired. "Why not Marianne's Memory?"

"Marianne wouldn't let me."

"Oh!" Charlie said. "So you've been in touch with her."

"She's my mum," the woman said. "She's in her seventies now. She was going to marry that pop star, the one in Brighton Peer. Giles Jessop. But she called it off at the last minute and ran off with his brother, Jeremy, the racing car driver. My dad. They live in the south of France, where I grew up. Anyway I asked her if I could use the name and she said no, and I'm dreadful with naming things and so I asked her, what should I call it then? And she said, just imagine something. And I said, I haven't got much of an imagination for things like that. And she said, well, it's easy when you know how. And that's how the shop got its name." She paused. "And you say your mother used to work here?"

"Yes," said Charlie. "She was friends with your mum. They shared a flat together, too. And I work in a museum—I'm putting together a display of the Swinging Sixties and I can see some of the clothes you've got here would look amazing in it. Can we look around?"

"Yes, of course. I'm Sue. If you want any help, just ask."

"Giles failed to mention his very famous brother, Jeremy," Mr. Deeley said as he and Charlie investigated the racks of frocks and jackets at the front of the shop.

"I wonder why," Charlie mused. She lifted out a black mini-dress with a trumpet flare, printed all over with bright pop petal flowers, with a white collar and white cuffs. "I love this. And these."

She showed Mr. Deeley a pair of white opaque tights on a nearby rack full of stockings and leg coverings.

"And the correct shoes," Mr. Deeley said thoughtfully, examining some shelves beside the sofa. He held up a pair of white t-bar leather Mary Janes.

"Salvatore Ferragamo," Sue supplied. "Genuine leather, made in Italy. Kitten heels. Perfect with that frock. You have an excellent eye for fashion."

"I should love to see you wearing these things," Mr. Deeley decided. "Might you change into them, to show them off...for me?"

"What, now?"

"Indeed," said Mr. Deeley. "My curiosity has been aroused."

Charlie laughed. "You too, then," she decided, selecting a mod-looking tie from the rack, in a floral and paisley pattern of red ochre, goldenrod yellow, bright aqua, and muted pink.

"John Stephen," Sue said. "Very nice. Would go with this, I think." She produced a wool suit, dark grey, beautifully tailored. "Hardy Amies. You can't do better than that."

"The waistcoat only," Mr. Deeley decided, removing it from its hanger. "Thank you. I shall retain my own trousers and boots."

They emerged from the single dressing room together, and stood in front of the large, elaborate mirror. "The very picture of a trendy 1960s couple," Sue judged. "Mum would have hired you on the spot."

Charlie laughed as Mr. Deeley made final adjustments to his tie.

It was a skill he'd only recently acquired. "We'll take them," Charlie said. "Shall I put them in bags for you...?"

"Yes. Unless you want to wear your new togs on the train, Mr. Deeley?"

"I think I might."

"Well, I think I might change back into my own clothes. This frock is lovely but it's far too short to be practical. I don't know how they managed back then, reaching up for things, bending over..."

"I should imagine the view was breathtaking," said Mr. Deeley, admiring Charlie as she turned to go back to the dressing room. Sue totted up the sale and wrote it out on a vintage receipt pad.

"Mr. Deeley." It was Charlie, calling from the dressing room. And then, more urgently: "Mr. Deeley!"

He stepped through the beaded glass curtain.

"What is it, Mrs. Collins?"

Charlie was still wearing her mini-dress. "I feel...peculiar."

"What sort of peculiar?"

"I've felt it before. It's…" She grabbed her bag and her original clothing, then thrust Mr. Deeley's jacket into his hands and grabbed onto his arm. "…the feeling I get when something's about to happen…"

They were still standing in the dressing room. And it looked more or less the same, down to the glass beads shielding it from the main part of the shop. And the shop still smelled of patchouli and ylang-ylang and there was still music blaring from the jukebox at the back.

But it was not the same.

This was evident as soon as they stepped through the curtain of glass beads.

The shop had changed. In fact, it was nothing like the shop they entered. This shop had clothes hanging from racks and neatly folded on tables, yes, but it was crammed full of other things: guitars, and portable record players, cardboard record album covers, framed photographs, and posters. Two birdcages, each containing a large stuffed parrot, sat at opposite ends of the room. A grandfather clock stood in the corner. Hats and caps and boots and lots of umbrellas hung on racks around the walls.

There was a counter, and behind the counter were two young women, one a blonde, one a brunette, both with masses of long straight hair and fringes. The woman with the blonde hair was dressed in a simple green dress with large white flowers, its hem ending just above her knees. The brunette was slightly more daring, in a pink skirt that was somewhat shorter, and a matching sleeveless knitted top with a high neck.

"It's Mum," Charlie whispered. "I've seen photos of her when she was in her twenties. The one with the dark hair."

"Then the other must be Marianne," Mr. Deeley reasoned. "Have we arrived in the fabulous Swinging Sixties?"

"It would seem so, Mr. Deeley. I'll just confirm the date."

Leaving her bundle of clothing with Mr. Deeley, Charlie approached the counter, where Marianne was engaged in a conversation with Charlie's mum.

"You should just go along and stand in the crowd," Marianne was urging. "You never know—you might catch a glimpse of one of them."

"Some of us aren't quite as lucky as you," Charlie's mum replied. "Some of us aren't going out with dishy pop stars. Say hello to Paul McCartney for me, won't you."

"Oh, Jackie. You know I'd take you with me if I could. Giles only just managed to get two tickets. He did ask if there were more."

"I believe you," Charlie's mum said. "Thousands wouldn't." She turned to Charlie. "Hello. I like your frock. Where's it from?"

"Um," Charlie said. "A little boutique. Easy When You Know How."

"I've never heard of that one, have you?" Jackie said to Marianne.

"I haven't, but I like the name," Marianne said thoughtfully.

"You're probably going to think I'm daft," Charlie said, "but can you tell me what day it is?"

"Wednesday," Marianne answered easily. "Happens to me all the time. I woke up this morning thinking it was Monday."

"No you didn't," Jackie said. "You woke up this morning shouting, 'Today's the day I'm going to meet the Beatles!'" She looked at Charlie. "Some people have all the luck, eh?"

"Some people," Charlie agreed. "Where's this fab meeting going to take place?"

"You really are out of it, aren't you," Marianne said. "Tonight. Just down the road at the London Pavilion."

"The premiere of their film," Jackie added. "*A Hard Day's Night.*"

"Ah..." Charlie said. "Yes. Of course. July the...er..."

"July the 6th," Marianne provided.

"1964," Jackie said humorously.

"They're expecting Princess Margaret and Lord Snowdon. Fifteen guineas a ticket."

"Yes, I know," Jackie said. "And a stuffy old champagne supper party afterwards at The Dorchester and then on to the Ad Lib Club for some late-night hobnobbing with the Rolling Stones. I myself will be enjoying a blind date with a bloke Marianne's boyfriend went to school with. Not quite the same as consorting with Antony Armstrong-Jones, but I'm told he's just as good-looking."

"He is," Marianne said, confidentially, to Charlie. "I've met him. Justin Duran. Isn't that the most fab name? All terribly aristocratic and French-sounding. He isn't, of course. He's English. From Stoneford. But he's quite dishy. If I wasn't already spoken for I'd definitely go for him."

"Justin Duran," Mr. Deeley said, thoughtfully, to Charlie. "This name is very familiar."

"Oh! Do you know him too?" Marianne said.

. "Indeed. I also attended school with him."

Charlie gave Mr. Deeley a look.

"Top bloke," Mr. Deeley continued. "I recall he excelled in the study of Latin, and World Geography, and had committed to memory Lacroix's *Differential and Integral Calculus*. In English, and in the original French."

"There you are," Marianne said to Jackie. "A gentleman *and* a scholar. You can't do better than that!"

━━━━◆○◆━━━━

Outside the boutique, Charlie burst into laughter. "That was my dad they were talking about!"

"Hence the familiarity."

"You're mad! She's going to tell him all about you, and they'll both know you're completely insane!"

"Then they will conclude that I am a rogue and a madman, who enjoys playing pranks upon unsuspecting young ladies."

"Perhaps he won't remember you."

"Why should it matter?"

"Because of the future, Mr. Deeley. Our future. You've never actually met my dad...the opportunity's never presented itself. But I've sent him photos, obviously...and I've talked about you a lot with him, and mentioned your name...I wonder if he's wondered about you..."

"I should think, Mrs. Collins, that it would be your mother who ought to remember. I *have* met her. And yet, she has no recollection of seeing me before. Unlike your grandmother, who did recall our meeting, but kept it a secret until her death. Do you not think this peculiar?"

Charlie was deep in thought. "Yes. That's very true. Mum ought to have remembered."

She looked up and considered the road, with its narrow pavement on both sides, and two lanes of cars crammed in between, and everywhere, people, young and curious, their eyes filled with adventure, their faces reflecting the optimism of the very beginning of the Swinging Sixties.

"What are we doing here, Mr. Deeley? Was it John Lennon's plectrum? Is that what brought us back to 1964?"

"Perhaps," Mr. Deeley said. They were walking north, towards Oxford Street. "Perhaps," he continued, "we are simply becoming more accustomed to the ability. I have discovered that if I wish it so, it becomes so. The plectrum was a lens for your thoughts. As was the shop, when we went inside. Did you wish to come here?"

"Not consciously," Charlie said as they passed the brown and white gables of Liberty and walked up Argyll Street. "Palladium," said Mr. Deeley, reading the golden letters spread across the tops of a collection Corinthian columns.

"Very famous. And Grade II listed. This, Mr. Deeley, is where Beatlemania began. Sunday, the 13th of October, 1963."

"Fascinating," said Mr. Deeley, who knew about the Beatles because he'd asked Charlie one evening about a song he'd heard, *Please Please Me*, and Charlie had told him to look it up. And he had. For three days.

"Is there a purpose to it all, Mr. Deeley?"

"To Beatlemania? Most definitely. There would be no premiere of *A Hard Day's Night* this evening without it."

Charlie smiled. "You know what I mean. Is there a purpose to our time travelling? We've done this three times before...and each time, it was for a reason. We did something. We influenced something that would otherwise have been un-influenced. What's the purpose of this journey?"

"Perhaps," said Mr. Deeley, "this has something to do with the child. The half-sibling you didn't know existed. Perhaps this is when he or she came to be."

"Perhaps not a half-brother or sister at all. Perhaps a full brother or sister," Charlie said. "My mum's going to meet my dad for the first time tonight. But she didn't actually marry him until 1969. Perhaps their circumstances just didn't allow them to marry before that...and she had to give the baby up for adoption. The time we're in now, Mr. Deeley, is very different from the time we came from, when it comes to unmarried women and their babies. It would have been so difficult for her."

Charlie stopped. She stopped because Mr. Deeley had stopped, and was observing a little man on the pavement just ahead of them. He looked to be about fifty, with round, wire-framed spectacles. He wore black trousers and an old-fashioned pullover vest, underneath which was a white shirt, with rolled-up sleeves. He was playing something Celtic

on a battered fiddle with exceptional skill, his violin case open on the
pavement in front of him for the collection of coins.

"A busker," Charlie provided. "Usually found in Underground
stations...but not all that uncommon on the surface. I expect the
police will ask him to move along."

"I am acquainted with this gentleman," Mr. Deeley replied. "He is
Fenwick Oldbutter."

"The time traveller?" Charlie said. "Ruby Firth gave me his business card..."

"And I consulted him, in matters to do with the interference of
history." He approached the little man. "Good day, sir. Have we
crossed paths by design, or by accident?"

Fenwick Oldbutter completed his tune. "The word 'accident' appears in my lexicon infrequently," he replied.

"Then by design," Mr. Deeley said. "Allow me to introduce Charlotte Duran."

Fenwick Oldbutter's eyes were bright.

"The love of your life. So pleased to meet you at last, my dear. And
happy that you did not, after all, perish in the Blitz. Are you hungry?"

Charlie realized that she was, indeed, quite hungry. They had left
Giles Jessop's flat just after two. It was now, unaccountably, nearly
five.

"There's a hamburger restaurant round the corner," Fenwick said.
"I frequent it often. Do join me. My treat."

The restaurant, near Oxford Circus, was not overly busy. The
waitresses wore black frocks with white collars, and the tables were
stocked with little grey pots of hot English mustard, and tomato-shaped plastic sauce holders.

"Just wait till the Yanks invade in a few years' time," Fenwick
said, as their burgers arrived, on china plates with a paper napkin
underneath. "I shan't bother to warn them."

"Indeed," said Mr. Deeley, applying a liberal layer of mustard to his
hamburger. "It is not within your remit to warn anyone of anything,
as I recall." He added mustard to Charlie's hamburger as well. "He
belongs to the same circle of travellers as Mrs. Firth. And he, also, has
undertaken the oath of non-interference. Although our meeting, by
design, would seem to contradict his intentions."

"Did you know we were going to arrive?" Charlie asked, scraping off most of the hot mustard that Mr. Deeley had added to her hamburger and replacing it with ketchup from the squeeze bottle.

"Are you in possession of the plectrum which lately belonged to John Lennon?" Fenwick asked.

Charlie looked at him, then checked her handbag.

"Yes," she said. She paused. "Did you know Giles Jessop was going to give it to me?"

Fenwick said nothing, instead choosing to sip from his cup of tea.

"Giles Jessop is a time traveller as well?" Charlie asked.

"Let us call him a sympathetic friend. And let us also recall the knowledge I imparted to your companion, Mr. Deeley, upon another very similar occasion. The power of suggestion is your strongest ally. Your imagination was engaged. It was your own imagination which brought both of you back to this time. Nothing more, and nothing less."

"But we are here for a reason. Each journey we've undertaken has had consequences, which were brought about by our actions," Charlie pressed.

"Your interrogation of Mr. Oldbutter will, I fear, be in vain, Mrs. Collins," Mr. Deeley replied. "His infuriating adherence to the Overarching Philosophy and his steadfast loyalty to the oath prevents him from confirming anything."

"I may, however, be persuaded to discuss," Fenwick added, inscrutably. "And possibly, to suggest."

Charlie contemplated her own cup of tea.

"Have you a suggestion, then, Mr. Oldbutter?"

"I do, in fact. It would not be in anyone's best interests if Jackie Lewis were to go out with Justin Duran this evening."

"Sorry," Charlie said, "but that's my dad. They have to meet. Or I won't be born."

"The mere fact that you exist at this moment and are here, enjoying a hamburger with me and your esteemed companion, indicates to me that they did, at some point, meet," Fenwick replied humorously. "I merely suggest that it should not be tonight. When are they married?"

"1969."

"There you are then. Five years in which to discover one another. I suspect not even you know the circumstances of their first meeting."

"I've never actually asked."

"And your brother and sister?"

"I don't think they know either. It's never really come up in conversations."

"What, then, if I were to tell you, that tonight is the only opportunity your mother will have to meet Tony Quinn?"

"Who's he?"

Fenwick turned his quizzical gaze to Mr. Deeley. "A relation of yours, I believe."

"I have not heard of him."

"Perhaps, then, you simply haven't had the opportunity to explore your family tree this far into the 20th century. He is a direct descendant of your son, Thaddeus Quinn. In the year we now occupy, he plays music. On the radio. He is what you might refer to as a pirate."

"Oh!" said Charlie. "On board a pirate radio ship. I know about those."

"Unfortunately," Fenwick said, "he will die, quite tragically, aboard that same ship. Quite soon. But tonight he will be attending the premiere of *A Hard Day's Night*. He will be late...and rushing to get inside."

"Why is it so important for my mum to meet him?" Charlie asked.

She stopped, and looked at Mr. Deeley. "Oh."

"Oh, indeed," Mr. Deeley replied, and they both looked at Fenwick.

"It is true that a child will be born early next year," Fenwick said. "And that child will grow up to be someone rather important."

"Who?" Charlie asked.

"I am not at liberty to reveal that."

"And why us?"

"I cannot say."

"You might say," Mr. Deeley said, "by the means of your powers of suggestion. You might even make arrangements. Or you might procure a favour. You can say, but you merely wish not to. Another of your more infuriating habits."

"I might procure a favour from the two of you," Fenwick deferred.

"Out of everyone currently in London," Charlie replied. "Why us?"

"Out of everyone currently in London, you are the closest to Jackie Lewis...and you, Charlotte, out of everyone in London, have the most to lose if your mother fails to meet Tony Quinn this evening."

"What do I have to lose?" Charlie persisted. "This is about the birth of a child, my half-sister or brother. Not me."

"Perhaps I might show you a small story from tomorrow's *Daily Chronicle*..."

Fenwick withdrew a yellowed newspaper clipping from his trouser pocket, and handed it across the table to Charlie.

It was very short story, about a traffic accident in Central London involving a Vespa and a lorry. The two passengers aboard the little motorcycle were killed instantly. The lorry driver was unhurt, but was being treated for shock. The accident victims were identified as Jacqueline Lewis, of Stanhope Gardens, South Kensington, and Justin Duran, of Earl's Court, both aged 23.

Stunned, Charlie showed the article to Mr. Deeley, who read it with great thought, and then handed it back to Fenwick.

"And this will happen tonight?" he said.

"This will happen," Fenwick replied, "unless something else happens, which will prevent it."

"But this newspaper story is from tomorrow. It *did* happen," Charlie countered.

Fenwick remained silent as he returned the clipping to his trousers pocket.

"Perhaps," Mr. Deeley mused, "that newspaper article has its origins in another reality."

"But I'm here," Charlie objected. "So that accident couldn't have happened...could it?"

"Who is to say what reality you might return to?" Fenwick replied. "Perhaps you will be unable to return at all, if, in fact, you no longer exist. I believe this to be a paradox you ought not to risk. Consider the consequences. You might vanish." He finished his cup of tea. "And then where would that leave your poor Mr. Deeley?"

"I have encountered this situation previously," Mr. Deeley said, "and given a choice, I should prefer not to have to deal with it again. I suggest we interfere, Mrs. Collins. Lest you suddenly cease to be, and cause me untold grief for another lifetime."

"Let us hope the boutique is still open," Mr. Deeley said, as they ran back through Soho, and down Carnaby Street, "and that your mother has not yet gone home."

His hope was in vain.

The door to Marianne's Memory was locked, a "Closed" sign hanging crookedly in its window.

"No!" Charlie cried, hammering on the glass.

There was movement from within, and moments later, Marianne appeared.

"We're closed!" she mouthed, through the window, pointing at the sign.

"Please let us in!" Charlie shouted. "It's terribly important! Please!"

Marianne hesitated, then relented, unlocking the door and admitting them to the darkened shop.

"You're lucky I was just totting up the accounts in the back. What's up?"

"We are in urgent need of Justin Duran's mobile number," Mr. Deeley replied. "We must contact him."

Charlie gave him a dig in the ribs with her elbow.

"Sorry," she said, "my friend means his telephone number. He's got a peculiar way of phrasing things."

"I don't know his number," Marianne said. "He's only just moved here from Stoneford. He came for a job in the city."

"What about Giles?" Charlie asked.

Marianne telephoned her boyfriend.

"Right, ok. Thanks, love. We'll give it a try."

She hung up the phone.

"Giles only has his number at work. He hasn't got a phone at his flat. He pops out and uses the call box at the end of the road."

"Is it too late to ring him at work?" Charlie said desperately. "I'll try," Marianne said, dialling the number. She waited. "No, no answer. It's gone half past five."

"What about Jackie?" Mr. Deeley inquired. "Will she be at home by now? Can we ring her?"

"I'm so sorry. We don't have a phone either. We've ordered one, but the Post Office takes ages to get round to installing them." She looked at Charlie and Mr. Deeley. "What is it? Is it a matter of life and death?"

"It is, actually," Charlie said. "What time is she meeting Justin?"

"Half past six." Marianne looked at her watch. "You've got time to catch them. Take the tube from Piccadilly Circus to Gloucester Road. We're in Stanhope Gardens. I'll give you the address."

As they raced through the back streets of Soho, down toward Piccadilly Circus, Mr. Deeley said: "Why did you nudge me, Mrs. Collins?"

"No mobiles, Mr. Deeley. They didn't show up properly till the 1990s. They're still tethered by landlines here. Look at all the red call boxes."

They emerged at the bottom end of Regent Street and ran towards the nearest Underground entrance. Across the road, where the fountain was, they could see crowds beginning to gather, and workers erecting metal barricades, while a huge marquee over the entrance to the London Pavilion proclaimed the presence of The Beatles in *A Hard Day's Night*.

"The fountain has moved," Mr. Deeley said, preventing Charlie from going down the stairs into the tube station.

"What?"

"The fountain topped with the Angel of Christian Charity. It is over there, in the centre of the road. I distinctly recall it being just over here in the time we have come from. Are we indeed inhabiting an alternate reality, Mrs. Collins?"

"No," Charlie said, "no...Mr. Deeley. I wish we were in an alternate reality, but they reconstructed this area in the late 1980s and moved the fountain. Everything's as it should be. Come on, we haven't got much time."

Beneath Piccadilly Circus lay the circular concourse of the Underground station.

"Tickets," Charlie said. "Money. What have you got?"

Mr. Deeley checked his pockets. "Coins," he said, offering them.

Charlie pulled her change purse out of her bag. No notes. Only more coins.

"Damn," she said.

She picked through the money in the palm of her hand.

"Five pence," she said. "Five new pence looks and weighs almost the same as an old sixpence. Excellent."

She took Mr. Deeley's coins and added her own, located a machine and bought two tickets for Gloucester Road. The machine dropped several old pennies in change into the metal tray. Charlie collected them and grabbed Mr. Deeley's hand. "This way to the Piccadilly Line," she said, pulling him towards the escalators.

⸺◆⸺

"There it is."

The flat Jackie and Marianne shared was on the top floor of a five-storey stuccoed 19th century terrace, painted white, with cast iron railings and Doric columns decorating its porches and cornices over its windows.

"Another building that's Grade II listed in our time, Mr. Deeley. Very posh indeed. It doesn't look too shabby in 1964, either. I wonder how mum and Marianne can afford it. I don't think the boutique brings in enough to pay the rent on this little lot."

"Perhaps," said Mr. Deeley, "Marianne's father would rather his daughter not be domiciled in a dwelling of lesser value. Might there be money in the family?"

"I think you're right, Mr. Deeley." Charlie rang the bell for Flat 5.

They waited.

"She can't have left yet. It's not even six."

A minute later, Jackie opened the big front door, slightly out of breath.

"Oh," she said. "I was expecting Justin." She looked at Charlie, and then at Mr. Deeley. "How did you know this is where I lived?"

"Marianne gave us your address," Charlie said. "Can we come inside?"

The flat was tiny, on the very top floor of the building, and reached by way of a very long climb up five flights of narrow stairs.

"I think it's where the servants must have once lived," Jackie said. "Marianne's bedroom's a bit larger than mine. And you can see where they've put in a little kitchen and an even littler loo. Now what's this all about?"

In the tiny sitting room, Charlie and Mr. Deeley sat down on a sofa that looked as if it had originally come from a French bordello.

"You're going to think we're bonkers..." Charlie began.

"...but we are travellers in time," Mr. Deeley finished.

Charlie looked at him. And then at Jackie.

"Been smoking a bit of the weedy stuff, have you?" Jackie replied, amused. "Marianne and Giles are mad about it. It just puts me to sleep, I'm afraid."

"I do not smoke," Mr. Deeley replied.

"Anything," Charlie added. "We really are time travellers, Jackie. We're from 2014. In fact, I'm..." She paused again, and glanced at Mr. Deeley for help. Almost imperceptibly, he shook his head.

"You're what?" Jackie said. "Trippy? Or just bonkers?"

"We have come to warn you," Mr. Deeley replied. "It would be a grave error if you were to meet Mr. Duran tonight and ride away on his motorbike."

"He hasn't got a motorbike," Jackie said.

As she spoke, the bell from the front door downstairs sounded. Jackie went over to the sitting room window, which overlooked the main road and the leafy square that gave the road its name. Charlie and Mr. Deeley followed.

Down below, they could see a young man with his hair cut and combed into fringe, long in the front and long in the back, pacing nervously on the pavement. There was a gunmetal-grey Vespa with burgundy seats parked on the road behind him. The young man gave up pacing, and instead perched on the padded seat of the little motorcycle.

Charlie clung to Mr. Deeley's arm. "It's my dad," she whispered. "He's so young."

"He didn't tell me about a motorbike," Jackie said. "I'm not sure I want to ride pillion on that. It's completely impractical."

She looked down at her skirt, which was blue, and very short and narrow, and clung to her hips and legs.

"You must make an excuse," Mr. Deeley urged.

"Please," Charlie pleaded.

"Why?" Jackie asked.

"There will be an accident," Mr. Deeley said, simply. "And you will die."

Jackie stared at him. "How can you know that?" she whispered.

"We've been sent to warn you," Charlie said.

"Perhaps if you were to consider us your guardian angels," Mr. Deeley suggested gently, "it might be easier for you to understand. And accept."

Jackie looked out of the window again, then darted out of the flat and ran down the stairs. Charlie and Mr. Deeley watched as she rushed out of the front door and onto the pavement, and spent some time talking to Justin, in earnest.

They watched as the expression on his face changed from curiosity, to disappointment, then to alarm and finally concern. They watched as he climbed aboard the Vespa and puttered away, and Jackie came back upstairs.

"I've made a date with him for next Saturday," she said, shutting the door behind her. "And to be on the safe side, we're going by bus. He borrowed the Vespa from his mate at work." She looked out of the window, thoughtfully. "He seems rather nice."

"Oh, he is!" Charlie assured her. "He won't stay working in London though. After you marry him, you'll move back to Stoneford, and he'll be quite a successful estate agent. And then you'll both retire to Portugal."

Jackie laughed. "Bloody hell," she said. "Stoneford! I don't think so. And Portugal! I'm terrible with foreign languages. Can't we just retire to Brighton or Bognor and run a little bed and breakfast place for tourists? That's more my style."

"You'll see," Charlie mused.

"Any kids, while you're predicting my future?"

"Oh yes. Three."

"Four," Mr. Deeley corrected.

"Yes," Charlie said quickly. "Four. I forgot."

"Well, now that you've managed to successfully disrupt my date with the man you're convinced I'm going to marry...what am I meant to do now?"

"Perhaps," said Mr. Deeley, "you might consider attending the premiere of that film in Piccadilly Circus."

"What, *A Hard Day's Night*? I haven't got a ticket."

"Neither do we," Charlie said. "What, a pair of guardian angels and you can't manage a couple of tickets to the hottest film premiere in London?"

"Our employer dislikes the Beatles," Mr. Deeley replied humorously. "He prefers the classical music of Mendelssohn, the *Hebrides Overture* in particular, and the *Italian Symphony*."

Charlie looked at him. "I didn't know you knew about Mendelssohn."

"There is much you don't know about me, Mrs. Collins. Do I surprise you?"

"Yes. Constantly."

"Do you dislike it?"

"Not at all. You may continue to surprise me for as long as you wish, Mr. Deeley." Charlie turned to Jackie. "I think we should go and stand in the crowd outside the theatre and watch the celebrities arrive. We might still manage to see the Beatles."

"I think I'd rather be with Giles and Marianne. They're actually going inside and managing to *meet* the Beatles." Jackie picked up her jacket, and her handbag. "Come on then. I'm all dressed up with nowhere else to go. You owe me dinner afterwards, though. Justin was going to take me somewhere very posh and very nice. And I'm starving."

———•◦•———

They surfaced, once more, at Piccadilly Circus, and attempted to climb the steps that led straight up from the underground concourse to the pavement in front of the Pavilion. But the exit was blocked, and through the barricade they could see a massive gathering of people, held back by a line of police.

"Come on," Jackie said. "This station's got more than one way out."

She ran around the circular concourse, past the public toilets, to the long passageway that led up into the old original Underground station building on Coventry Street. When they reached the surface, they saw a line of spectators had spilled over onto a slender paved traffic island in the middle of Coventry Street, which was surrounded by a metal fence.

"Never mind that," Jackie said. "Follow me."

She dashed across the road, dodging a bus and three cars, followed closely by Charlie and Mr. Deeley.

"Takes me back to school, this," Jackie said, impetuously, clambering over the island barricade in her mini-skirt. "Pardon my knickers."

"They are most fetching," Mr. Deeley remarked as he climbed over the railings himself, and, with practiced but unnecessary chivalry, assisted Charlie.

The line of spectators was three or four people deep on the paved island, and they all seemed to be much taller than Charlie or Jackie, although Mr. Deeley could easily see over their heads.

On the Pavilion side of the road, a striped tent had been erected from the curbside to the theatre's entrance. A line of policemen stood to the left of this, holding back another throng of spectators. Other police with huge white cuffs directed important-looking black cars to the front of the tent.

A loud cheer came from the crowd as one such car drove up and stopped, and several people climbed out.

"Who is it?" Charlie asked Mr. Deeley.

"I cannot be certain," he said. "However, I do not believe it is Mendelssohn."

Charlie turned to ask Jackie, but Jackie had disappeared.

"Can you see Jackie?" she asked Mr. Deeley.

Mr. Deeley scanned the crowd on the traffic island.

"I cannot," he said.

"Bloody hell."

Charlie dug her way through to the row of people lining the barricade facing the Pavilion. "Let me through!" she demanded, ducking under arms and cameras and bags, "I'm little! And I've lost my mum!"

She reached the front just as another car drew up, and a man climbed out, accompanied by a woman with long blonde hair.

The people around her began to shout and cheer and aim their cameras.

"John! John! Cyn! Here! Over here!"

John Lennon, Charlie thought, all worries about Jackie momentarily banished. *I've just seen John Lennon.* She remembered the plectrum in her bag, and hugged it a little bit closer to her body.

But then. Jackie. Where was she?

And she realized, too late, that she'd also lost Mr. Deeley. Hemmed in by people who were all at least six inches taller than she was, it was impossible to see where he was.

I will not panic. She hated crowds. This was such a stupid idea. *I will not panic. Where is he?*

Her attention was diverted by a commotion on the other side of the road. Behind the police barricade, beside the blocked entrance to the tube station, very near to the striped tent, a young woman, obviously unconscious, her arms dangling limply, was being handed over the heads of the onlookers. With her heart in her throat, Charlie recognized Jackie's long dark hair and her short blue miniskirt.

"Oh God—no!"

She was hemmed in on all sides. There was no way to get to Jackie except over the barricade, across the road, and over a second metal fence preventing pedestrians from doing exactly what she was now attempting.

Charlie ran around three stopped cars, two motorbikes, and four policemen. One tried to reach out and grab her. She shook him off, and clambered over the last barricade, and elbowed her way through the crowd until she found herself on other side of the road.

Jackie wasn't there.

She was, however, about twenty feet away, lying on a piece of pavement where there were no people, other than a well-dressed man who was talking to her, attempting to bring her around, and a policeman who was keeping the area clear of bystanders.

"Is she all right?" Charlie asked desperately, running to Jackie's side.

"I think so," the man replied. "She's still breathing. She's got a nice strong pulse. She's not hurt." He glanced at his watch. "We've called for an ambulance."

"Jackie," Charlie said, kneeling on the ground beside her. "Remember me?"

Jackie opened her eyes, slowly, and tried to focus on Charlie. "What's happened?"

"You fainted," said the man. "Fortunately I was nearby and caught you before you were trampled. I made sure you were carried to safety. You all right, love?"

"I fainted?"

"Yes, love. It can happen to anyone."

"Where am I?"

"Piccadilly Circus," the man said. "Outside the London Pavilion."

"Did I go to work today?"

"Yes, you did," Charlie said.

"Why am I here?"

"Premiere of *A Hard Day's Night*. Remember?"

"I don't remember," Jackie said, her face filled with confusion. "Who're you?"

"I'm Charlie. We met in your shop. I came to your flat with Mr. Deeley."

"I don't remember." Jackie said again. She looked at the man. "Who're you?"

"Tony Quinn, love. What's your name?"

"Jackie Lewis."

Why doesn't Jackie remember me? Charlie thought. "Did you hit your head when you fell?" she asked.

"She didn't," Tony replied. "I caught her before she went all the way down."

"What year is it?" Charlie asked her.

Jackie thought, but came up blank. "I don't know."

"But you do know your name?"

"Yes. Jacqueline Elizabeth Lewis."

"And when were you born?"

"January the 23rd, 1941."

She tried to sit up, but Tony Quinn made her lie back down on the pavement. "You stay like that, love, until the ambulance comes."

"What's happened?"

"You fainted, love. Outside the London Pavilion."

"I fainted?"

"Yes, love."

"Where am I?"

"Piccadilly Circus," Charlie repeated.

"Did I go to work today?"

"Yes, you did."

"Why am I here?"

Charlie looked again at the well-dressed gentleman who was kneeling on the pavement beside Jackie, holding her hand.

"It's some kind of amnesia," she said. "But it doesn't make sense...she knows her name and her birthday. She just doesn't remember anything that's happening right now."

"My sister had this," Tony Quinn said. "She was coming down with something, her body was fighting some kind of infection, and she was terribly worried about her son, who was having a bit of trouble at school...she woke up in the morning and couldn't remember a thing from Monday onward. Exactly the same as this. We'd say something to her and she wouldn't recall it two minutes later. No retention at all. She asked the same questions over and over again. We thought she'd had a stroke, but the doctor at the hospital said no. Called it something very technical. Let me think."

He paused.

"Transient global amnesia. She recovered from it completely. But she never did get her memory back from that week."

"What's happened?" Jackie asked for the third time as the ambulance finally arrived.

The ambulance had gone, speeding away with its blue lights flashing and its bell ringing. Tony Quinn had climbed into the back with Jackie, vowing to see her safely to the hospital—something he deemed far more important than attending the premiere of *A Hard Day's Night* and meeting the Beatles for the fourth or possibly the fifth time.

"Anyway," he said as the ambulance door closed, "McCartney owes me ten quid from the last blast we were at. See you again, I hope, Charlie."

And he was gone, along with Jackie.

Charlie stood alone on the pavement. The crowds had thinned considerably, and it was dark. All of the Beatles had arrived and gone inside, along with a procession of celebrity friends. Traffic was flowing normally again along Coventry Street.

"Anyway," she repeated, to herself. "Mission accomplished. Accidentally, but nonetheless accomplished. Mum has met Tony Quinn. My half-sibling will be born."

She looked for Mr. Deeley, but couldn't find him.

A terrible thought came over her...what if he had tried to go back to their present, without her, got lost somewhere along the way, and couldn't find his way home? She might never see him again. He might be lost forever, wandering in time. And what if she couldn't get back either? She'd never tried to deliberately travel by herself. She'd left all that experimentation to Mr. Deeley.

Her common sense told her she should stay put, and wait here at Piccadilly Circus until Mr. Deeley reappeared. But, for how long? It might be hours. Days.

Years.

She might end up like one of those waifs they sang about in folk songs, wandering in solitude, waiting in vain for a lover who never came back.

She was, indeed, wandering in solitude. Almost without noticing, she had wandered all the way back to Oxford Street, to the hamburger restaurant where she and Mr. Deeley had met Fenwick Oldbutter.

It was open, its warm yellow lights beckoning through large plate glass windows.

Charlie went inside, and sat down, half expecting Fenwick to reappear and congratulate her for a job well done.

Fenwick did not reappear. A waitress did, however, and Charlie ordered a hamburger and a cup of tea, realizing, as she did, that she had absolutely no way to pay for it. Her collection of coins would be as foreign to the cashier as French francs or American dimes and quarters. There was an American Express sticker on the door, but she didn't have an American Express card. And the banks hadn't yet introduced their credit cards to England.

Her burger arrived, and her tea. Charlie added a squeeze of ketchup from the tomato-shaped dispenser and waited.

Two cups of tea later, and a plate of chips, she was still waiting. With an extremely guilty conscience, she contemplated making a run for it without paying for her meal. She'd never done anything like that in her life. It was a horrible thing to consider. But she'd already cheated the Underground. And she was thinking about cheating again.

And then what? Assuming she wasn't nabbed by the police... what? Go back to Stanhope Gardens and wait for Marianne to show up? Deliver the news about Jackie...ask if she could spend the night in her bed?

She was summoning up the courage to bolt when, at last, she saw Mr. Deeley.

He was looking very jaunty in his John Stephen tie and Hardy Amies waistcoat. He glanced through the big glass window, smiled as he spotted Charlie, then opened the door and came inside.

"Where have you been?" Charlie asked him as he sat down.

"I might ask you the same thing," Mr. Deeley replied, amused. He turned to the waitress who had arrived at Charlie's table almost as quickly as he had. "I shall have the same things to eat as my friend. Many thanks."

"I can't pay for any of this," Charlie whispered, when the waitress was out of earshot. "Old money."

"Old money," Mr. Deeley replied, removing a £10 note from his trousers pocket. "Happily, I can."

"Where did you get that?"

"I shall relate what happened after you abandoned me," Mr. Deeley replied.

"I was trying to find Jackie!"

"You left me alone," Mr. Deeley said, sounding slightly miffed. "I had no choice but to negotiate my way out of the crowd. Whereupon I crossed the road, and joined another crowd—albeit with a greatly reduced number of participants—and, within some moments, I discovered myself to be inside the building."

"Which building?" Charlie asked.

"The building where the film was to be shown."

"The London Pavilion? You were inside the London Pavilion?"

"Indeed."

"How the hell did you manage that, Mr. Deeley?"

His meal arrived and he paid the waitress, who brought back his change on a china plate. Infuriatingly, he paused to drink his tea and add hot mustard and ketchup to his hamburger before continuing the tale.

"I cannot say for certain," he replied inscrutably. "In any case, I went into the cinema, and saw that there were empty seats, and so I availed myself of one, and sat down to watch the film. It was very good, by the way. Have you seen it?"

"I have," Charlie said. "Four times. And where did you get the £10?"

"After the film finished, I found I was in need of the gentlemen's toilet. And so, after asking for directions, I repaired to the facilities, whereupon I found myself standing beside a Beatle."

"You met a Beatle in the loo?"

Mr. Deeley finished his tea. "And I engaged him in conversation about the film, and about being chased by a large number of screaming females through a railway station. I also asked him how he managed to disappear from the bath."

"John Lennon. You met John Lennon in the loo. You talked to John Lennon about *A Hard Day's Night*." "I did, in fact. And then I explained our circumstances, that we had only recently arrived in London, and that we were, unhappily, without sufficient funds for a meal. He gave me that £10 note."

"You spare changed John Lennon in the loo for ten quid."

"And I told him we had one of his plectrums."

"What did he say?"

"He was amused. He gave me another."

Mr. Deeley removed the plectrum from the pocket of his trousers and held it out in the palm of his hand.

"He just happened to have it with him," Charlie said.

"He did. And three more. Imagine that."

Charlie smiled.

"He wished me good fortune for the future, and I wished him the same, and we parted as friends. He struck me as a very nice fellow."

"Mr. Deeley," Charlie said. "You have no idea, do you?"

"Do I not...?"

Charlie shook her head. She took out the plectrum that was in her bag, and placed it in Mr. Deeley's palm, beside its twin. She took his other hand in hers.

"Do you think we could go home now...?"

It was still a hamburger restaurant. But its wooden tables and chairs had been replaced by bright plastic, and the waitresses had been replaced by a long counter, with an equally long lineup of hungry patrons queuing in front of four cash registers. There was music coming from somewhere, and the lights were glaringly bright.

"This seems a much simpler process than our previous journey," Mr. Deeley remarked. "Easy when you know how."

"Let's find a posh hotel and spend the night in London," Charlie said. "It's probably too late to get a train back to Middlehurst anyway."

"Will it have a very large and comfortable bed, with feather pillows and a bath which is big enough for two?" Mr. Deeley mused.

"I think that could certainly be arranged."

"Then do arrange it, Mrs. Collins. I am feeling particularly amorous after this day's adventures."

Charlie smiled, and kissed him. "Can't wait." She paused. "I wonder who my mum's son or daughter will turn out to be."

"If it is a descendant of mine, he or she is bound to be indescribably fascinating."

Charlie laughed, and took out her mobile. "I must look up transient global amnesia. Mum's never mentioned any of this to us."

"Perhaps," Mr. Deeley said, "it is better that she has not ever recalled this day. How will you arrange for our hotel?"

Charlie searched on her mobile and rang a number.

"We'll be there in about twenty minutes," she said.

She put her mobile back in her bag.

"Easy when you know how," she said, plucking the two plectrums out of Mr. Deeley's still open palm.

ABOUT EASY WHEN YOU KNOW HOW...

This is another Charlie Duran / Shaun Deeley short story, this one taking place chronologically between *In Loving Memory* and the third book in the time travel series, *Marianne's Memory*. "Easy When You Know How" was included at the end of *In Loving Memory* to help set up the next book in the series.

The story draws upon a couple of my own experiences. It's 1964 and Charlie, Mr. Deeley and Jackie join the crowds at Piccadilly Circus for the premiere of the Beatles' film, *A Hard Day's Night*, at the London Pavilion. I wasn't at that particular event, but four years later, in the summer of 1968, I *was* at the premiere of *Yellow Submarine*. Same place—Piccadilly Circus—and the same theatre—the London Pavilion. I was somewhere in the crowd in the press photos from that evening, and I really did see all four Beatles arrive.

Outside the theatre, Jackie faints in the massive crush of people and wakes up suffering from Transient Global Amnesia. During a TGA episode, you have a sudden, temporary memory loss. You know basic things like who you and your family members are, but you can't form new memories and you have problems recalling things that happened recently. It's as though your brain is stuck in a loop of questions and answers, but nothing anyone tells you is retained.

TGA is a fairly rare condition but I know someone who has suffered from it not once, but twice! They were all right after a good night's sleep, but couldn't recall anything that had happened during the first episode, including a visit to the hospital's Emergency Room, and a thoroughly baffled doctor. TGA presents itself as something quite serious (though it isn't, really). I managed to find some humour in it, and worked it into "Easy When You Know How".

9

SALTY DOG BLUES

It was 2012, and I was working as an entertainer on board the *Star Sapphire*, a former ocean liner that had been repurposed by StarSea Cruises for the summer run between Vancouver and Alaska. Jason Davey, TopDeck Lounge, performing all your vocal and instrumental favourites, 8 till Late. My real last name's Figgis, but I have well-known musical parents, and back then—as now—I wanted to distance myself from their fame.

For lifesaving and accommodation purposes I was considered Crew. But for all social activities, including food and drink, I was the equivalent of an Officer. I enjoyed the freedom of the ship, upstairs and down.

All our guests had boarded, we'd done our mandatory Passenger Muster, and we were on our way to Juneau. I had about an hour before I was due onstage, so I went downstairs for an early supper.

"Detached retinas," said Barrie, our Chief Purser, as I sat down with my selection from the self-service buffet. Every evening in the Officers Mess the chefs picked the least popular item from the passenger menu and let us have it for dinner. That night it was Spaghetti Bolognaise. "That's a new one."

"Medical emergency?" I inquired.

"Miss Abigail Ferryman." Quentin, our Assistant Purser, a fine young lad from Scotland, hated spaghetti and had opted for a large plate of Caesar Salad with triple helpings of grated Parmesan. "She claims to have an allergy to the colour blue. She informed us it would cause her retinas to detach. Amongst other things. I've arranged to have all offending items removed from her cabin. Though the carpeting may prove to be a bit of a stumbling block."

"She's travelling with a service dog," Barrie added.

"For her allergy?" I also hated spaghetti but I had a three-hour gig ahead of me and I needed the carbs. I bribed myself by dousing it with some generous dollops of hot sauce.

"The wee doggie's name is Lord Fothergill," Quentin replied. "Though I've decided to call him Spike. If no one objects."

"Spike might," I said.

"'Wee' being the operative word this afternoon just after Sailaway," Barrie said. "Against a chair leg. In the Atrium Room."

"Offended by the décor?" I guessed. The principal colours in the Atrium Room were shades of green. No possibility of detached retinas.

"Bloody service dogs," Barrie muttered.

"I thought we provided special places for service dogs to...wee," I said.

"Oh, we do, Jason. But Lord Fothergill apparently has an easily irritated and very impatient bladder."

"That'll be Strike One then," Quentin said, humorously. "Failure to use the designated relief area. And with all due respect, Spike is not a true service dog. He merely provides emotional support."

"I'll be needing emotional support by the time we dock in Juneau," Barrie said.

<hr>

I went back to my cabin to change into my gigging togs. On the way, I walked past Seawind, the passenger dining room, to see if I could spot Spike and his owner.

It wasn't difficult. Miss Ferryman was a large woman with flowing red hair, wearing a royal purple khaftan with gold embroidery. Spike, a Chihuahua, was sporting a matching shirt and leggings, as well as a glittering gold collar embellished with a purple feather that looked like something he'd stolen from a stripper. Spike and his owner had availed themselves of a table near the door, and, Spike, standing on his hind legs on a chair, was happily chowing down on hamburger from our Sailaway Dinner Menu.

"'Evening," I said, to Marcello, our *maître d'*, who was giving Spike the evil eye.

"It is not a good evening at all," Marcello replied. "Chef Franco is livid. That...animal...has defiled his most favourite Sailaway creation."

"Really...?" Chef Franco had only been on board for three weeks, but already had a reputation for his inordinately fierce temper. Our Seawind Burger seemed hardly worth getting upset over.

"Seafood Turnover with Lobster Sauce," the *maître d'* continued. "He wolfed it down...and then..."

Marcello leaned towards me, confidentially.

"He...vomited!"

"Oh dear," I said. "Defiled indeed."

"His owner demanded more food. And so, what you see."

I *tsk'd* my sympathetic disapproval.

"And that...animal...should be on the floor."

"Check the chair legs after they leave," I suggested. "And ask House-keeping for stain and odour remover. Just a thought."

As I exited I could hear Spike snorting his opinion of Chef Franco's lobster sauce. As I opened the Crew Only door in the Seawind foyer, I heard something that sounded suspiciously like a water glass smashing. And as I walked down the stairs to my cabin I could hear Chef Franco's outraged baritone voice exclaiming something not very polite in broken English, punctuated with furious Italian.

Downstairs, it was noisy and claustrophobic, only a deck away from the Engine Room. One main thoroughfare with side passageways leading off to crew cabins, stores and utilities, the ship's laundry. Glaring fluorescents, overhead pipes, lino floors. The constant roar of the turbines. No portholes—we were down at the waterline. Watertight doors, ten of them, bow to stern. I was lucky—I had a cabin to myself. Others had to share.

I changed into a bright blue silk shirt, sleeves rolled fashionably up between wrist and elbow, and black trousers, and went back upstairs to play.

You don't see ships like the *Sapphire* anymore. SOLAS has done away with vessels that don't meet minimum safety requirements and passengers demand more activities and entertainment than we could ever have provided. She may have been old and creaky, but our little *Sapphire* had six times more character than those bang-for-buck floating resorts with eighteen passenger decks, nineteen restaurants, twenty pools, four water slides, a go-kart track and a golf course bolted on top of a barge.

As I waited for the passenger lift outside the Dining Room, I spotted a man and a woman in matching turquoise windbreakers trying to make sense out of the deck plan bolted to the wall.

"Can I help?" I inquired. "You Are Here."

I pointed out where we were. There had once been a red dot stuck to the diagram, but it had been worn away.

"We're trying to find our cabin," said the man.

"He forgot the map," said his wife. "He left it on the bed."

"What deck is your cabin on?" I asked.

"The one where the shops are," the woman replied.

The ship had eleven decks in total, though the bottom three were reserved for crew and the Engine Room. The Officers Mess and the Seawind Dining Room were on Deck 4—Caribe.

Deck 5—Baja—had passenger cabins and the Showcase Lounge, home of our nightly cabaret. Deck 6—Aloha—had more cabins and the Purser's Desk.

Deck 7—Promenade—was where our passengers boarded, and where the Atrium Room was—and the Shopping Arcade, which was located just outside the Atrium Room's entrance doors. And towards the Prom's bow were the "expensive" cabins—the ship's old First Class staterooms from her transatlantic days.

"There you are," I said, tapping the map. "Forward Prom. Up at the posh end."

"Thank you!" said the man. "Do you work on board?"

I showed him my name tag, which was in my trousers pocket and which I should have been wearing. But it gets in the way of my guitar, so I never put it on when I'm playing.

"TopDeck Lounge," I said. "I'm the featured entertainment."

"Do you do requests?" the woman asked, clearly impressed.

"Of course."

"Then we'll see you there!"

I rode in the lift with them as far as Prom, and then continued on my own to Deck 8—Lido—which had outside decks, an informal cafe and the Casino and then Deck 9—Sports—which was the home of the ship's library and, next to it, the TopDeck Lounge, where I was installed for your nightly listening pleasure.

We were directly underneath the Bridge, which was on Deck 10—Sun—and Deck 11—Observation—where you could always find the best views of the passing coastal wilderness and, if you were lucky, a whale or two.

———◆———

It was dark and we were zigzagging through Seymour Narrows—a passage Captain George Vancouver once called one of the vilest stretches of water in the world. That was when Ripple Rock still existed—an immense and inconvenient hazard which was removed in a planned explosion in 1958. But the tide in the Narrows can still top sixteen knots, which is why Alaska-bound cruise ships always try to beat it by leaving Vancouver a good few hours before sunset.

My job was to play my guitar and sing. I had assorted other trickery, including backing tracks, to enhance my performance and impress the guests.

It was past ten o'clock and most of the First Sitting post-meal passengers had drifted off to bed, replaced by Second Sitting, who tended to be younger, more energetic and less reliant on medications. I glanced over the audience as I worked through my usual assortment of Sailaway tunes.

There was Danny, the ship's photographer, off-duty and enjoying a drink with Diandra, one of the shoppies, still in her uniform—a white shirt with a distinctive little black and white silk scarf, and a black skirt, short and pencil-tight. Danny and Diandra had been an item for the past couple of months.

There was an anaemic-looking guy who was undergoing psychiatric counselling to help him get over his pathological fear of dogs (he'd said so in a very loud voice to Carla, that week's waitress, as she took his order).

And sitting at the table beside him, the couple wearing the matching turquoise windbreakers—who'd spent my entire set texting on their cellphones.

And then I spotted *them* walking into the room: Miss Ferryman with her royal purple khaftan and flowing red hair, and Spike, with his feather, looking for trouble.

The anaemic-looking guy bolted out of the lounge without finishing his drink as Carla placed a little glass dish of mixed bar snacks on Miss Ferryman's table.

"Bring us something else," Miss Ferryman demanded. "Lord Fothergill dislikes peanuts."

"I'm afraid we don't have anything else," Carla replied. And then: "Does he have an allergy?"

"Are you making fun of me? Lord Fothergill enjoys perfect health. Take this abomination away, remove the peanuts and bring it back."

Carla valued her job. "What can I get you to drink?" she inquired, placing the little dish on her tray.

"A Parfait d'Amour for me and an Evian Water for Lord Fothergill. Served at room temperature. In a china bowl."

"Would you mind putting your dog on the floor?" Carla asked.

"Lord Fothergill dislikes the floor. He prefers a chair."

"I'm really sorry, but service animals are not allowed to sit on the furniture. Also, he should be on a leash or a harness..."

Miss Ferryman stared at Carla.

"A Parfait d'Amour," she said, "and an Evian Water. Room temperature. In a china bowl."

Carla walked back to the bar.

I finished my song—"Beyond the Sea"—to a smattering of applause. Carla brought me a chilled melon juice—my favourite nightly tipple. I decided on "Sail On, Sailor", the Beach Boys' tune, while Carla returned the nut-less bar snacks to Miss Ferryman's table.

That's when Spike jumped down from his chair and trotted across to my setup in the middle of the dance floor.

"*Go away*," I said, under my breath, between verses.

But Spike was having none of it.

In fact, he decided to sing along. Loudly.

I seriously doubt Brian Wilson ever considered a howling Chihuahua when he co-wrote the lyrics for my vocal offering. I smoothly segued into something else by the Beach Boys that could accommodate a howl in Spike's key— "I Get Around"—and improvised a duet, which made my audience laugh.

Not content to simply join my act, Spike wandered around to the back of the stage to see if he could make it as a roadie.

"*Don't even think about it,*" I said.

But Spike was investigating my amp.

"*No!*" I said, in no uncertain terms. "*Bad dog!*"

But it was too late. Spike's leg was up...

There was a thunderous buzz as the fuse inside my amp shorted out...followed by limp silence from my guitar.

I'm not sure what "Fuck you, Jason" is in Chihuahua-speak, but it sounds a lot like "*yeyurp*" and there's a derisive snort at the end for added emphasis.

I stood up, retrieved Spike from the floor and carried him at arm's length, like a baby with a whiffy nappy, back to his owner.

"Your dog," I said, plopping him back on his chair.

"Lord Fothergill is impressed with your mastery of the guitar," Miss Ferryman replied. "Please do continue."

If that was admiration, I'd have loved to have seen what Spike did to musicians he hated.

I carried on my set with just my acoustic Gibson and a good deal of singing. By midnight, the lounge was empty, and I was serenading Samuel and Carla and Javier, a deck steward who'd sneaked in for three tins of Guinness and a nearly-full bottle of Blue Curacao. Javier was from Argentina and was disembarking for his six-weeks' leave on Monday when we docked in Juneau. He was obviously in a mood for early celebrations.

———◦———

"That animal," said Barrie, our Chief Purser, at breakfast, as he chowed down on stewed prunes and Special K, "will be the death of me."

"That animal will be the death of my show," I replied.

While I was having my scrambled eggs, sausage and toast, the ship's electricians were examining my amp. I had spare fuses. But Spike's piss must have contained some kind of secret Chihuahua corrosive. The wires, and everything else within three inches of his target, were shot.

Our conversation was interrupted by Quentin, who'd left ten minutes earlier to go to work, but had now rushed back.

"Sorry, sir," he said, to Barrie, "but you're wanted upstairs. It seems late last night the wee doggie was spotted in the aft jacuzzi and some of the guests have complained."

"Fucking hell," Barrie said, pushing back from the table.

"Can I come too?" I inquired.

Not only had Spike been enjoying a post-concert splash in the Promenade Deck hot tub—it seemed he'd also obviously decided it would be an excellent spot to have a bowel movement, and his contribution to the décor had been plopped prominently onto the jacuzzi's apron. Putting the poop back in poop deck, as it were.

The lineup at the Purser's Desk consisted of Javier (the unfortunate deck steward who'd been summoned to remove Spike's droppings), as well as Peter, the Head Pool Butler (who he reported to); Chef Franco and Marcello, both intent on lodging their complaints concerning Spike's dining habits; Diandra, the shoppie, who'd been chased around the jewellery counter as she'd closed up for the evening; Belinda, the Retail Sales Manager who looked after the entire Shopping Arcade and was nicknamed "The Dragon Lady", mostly because of her unsympathetic tirades towards her employees; and Diandra's boyfriend Danny, the photographer, who'd been pissed on as he'd put up all of yesterday's passenger embarkation shots in the Picture Gallery. There were also a handful of guests with harrowing tales of unsolicited contact, including the anaemic psychiatric patient, whose name, it transpired, was Mr. Bothwell; and the texting duo in the matching windbreakers who, it turned out, were called Mitch and Honey.

"I want you to know we'll be discussing this very serious disruption to our perfect holiday on Twitter and Facebook," Honey was saying, jabbing her cellphone into the air to make her point.

"I really wish you wouldn't," Barrie said. "And I hope you'll consider that we're working to resolve the problem to the best of our abilities and with our guests' health and comfort foremost in our efforts. I'll be extending each of you a $100 credit for drinks to show our appreciation for your patience and understanding."

I'd situated myself on the Aft Promenade, snaffling one of the wooden imitation steamer chairs and a couple of padded cushions while I checked Twitter on my phone.

It was a glorious Sunday and the passing scenery, as ever, was spectacular. We'd spent the night cruising Johnstone Strait and Discovery Passage. We were just about to adjust our course towards Triple Island where we'd exchange our Canadian pilots for ones from Southeastern Alaska.

I was scanning for disgruntled #starsapphire hashtags when a shadow fell over my little screen. I looked up. It was, of course, Quentin.

"Sorry to bother you, Jason, but Miss Ferryman's having a wee turn and she's asking for you."

"Why me?" I said.

"Apparently Spike's gone missing."

"And she thinks I had something to do with it?"

"Not at all. She's asking for your assistance."

"I don't understand. Why?"

"I believe it may have to do with some reluctance on the part of ship's security to launch an investigation. And the fact that she insists Spike has taken a strong liking to you. Will you come?"

I love a good mystery.

I knocked on Miss Ferryman's door.

"Who's that?"

"Jason Davey."

"Who?"

"The musician," I said, patiently. "You wanted to see me?"

"Yes! Come in."

Miss Ferryman's cabin was one of the former First Class staterooms up at the forward end of the Promenade Deck. It now looked anything but. The two large square windows overlooking our long bow were minus their curtains. The marine blue bedspread had been removed, exposing the tan brown blankets that were standard in all our cabins. Sheets had been draped over the two armchairs, and the entire floor was covered in a white tarpaulin that I'd last seen up near the funnel in Skagway, where the painters had been dealing with some rust.

Miss Ferryman had arranged herself on the bed in a pose reminiscent of something from a silent-era film where the dialogue text frame would have contained one word: *Distraught*.

Spike's bed—an upholstered purple indulgence—lay beside her pillow, forlorn and empty.

"Sit," she commanded, waving at a sheet-covered armchair.

I sat.

"I am unwell," she said.

"I'm sorry to hear that." I'd done the StarSea course in Customer Relations. They told us never to apologise for anything. I made a point of breaking the rule whenever I could.

"Lord Fothergill is missing."

"So I was told. But he can't have gone far."

"He's been abducted."

"Why do you think that?" I asked.

"Lord Fothergill would never deliberately leave my side. He is devoted to me."

"How is it he went missing, then?"

"We were taking our exercise along the Enclosed Promenade. I was momentarily distracted by the ship's photographer, who was attempting to take my picture for his ridiculous display board. After I dismissed him, I looked for Lord Fothergill. But he was gone."

"And what time was this?" I asked.

"Immediately after breakfast. Ten o'clock."

To my mind, 10 a.m. wasn't quite "immediately after breakfast". But to each his own.

"And you didn't have him on a leash?" I asked.

"Lord Fothergill despises confinement. Leashes create anxiety."

"And what was he wearing when you last saw him?" I inquired, imitating my favourite TV police procedurals in a lame attempt to humour her.

Miss Ferryman failed to be amused. "A red and white hand-knitted cardigan and a matching scarf. It was chilly on deck. And his feather, of course. It was a bequeathment from his grandfather, who received it as a gift from a prominent member of the Royal Family when he was awarded the Freedom of the Palace and the beloved friendship of Her Majesty's Corgis. Lord Fothergill always displays it on his collar."

"And you had a good look for him...?"

"Of course I did," Miss Ferryman snapped. "Do you take me for an idiot? I searched fruitlessly for over an hour."

"Is it possible," I said, carefully, "that he might have fallen overboard?"

"It is not," Miss Ferryman replied. "Lord Fothergill is a seasoned traveller. He's accompanied me on numerous cruises. He would not have gone anywhere near the railings."

"And what did you do next?"

"I went to see the Chief Purser. He referred me to your Chief Security Officer."

Our Chief Security Officer, Kevin Blaney, was sixty-three years old and trained in antiterrorism. He'd once done highly classified things with the British Navy. I was sure the thought of investigating a potential dognapping would thrill him to no end.

"Mr. Blaney informed me he would look into it. This isn't good enough. I want an investigation. Now."

"I'm not sure what you think I can do..."

"Lord Fothergill is very fond of you."

"He pissed on my amp," I said.

"As I informed you last night, it was an expression of his affection. He thinks the world of you. I wish you to intercede."

"I'm sure Mr. Blaney is doing his best to track him down."

"I'm sure he isn't," Miss Ferryman snapped.

"When the photographer was trying to take your picture this morning, do you remember if there was anyone else in the general vicinity?"

"Nobody. I was quite alone."

"Are you absolutely certain?"

Miss Ferryman considered me, and then said: "There was a woman from one of the shops. I saw her fleetingly."

"And you're sure she was from the shops?"

"Of course. I recognized her clothing."

"And what was she doing?"

"She was standing in the doorway. Looking out."

"The doorway that leads from the foyer to the Enclosed Promenade?"

"Yes. The very one."

"Was she doing anything else?"

"Not that I could see."

"Would you recognize her again?"

"I suppose I would."

"Could you come with me and point her out?"

It was inconvenient, of course. But Miss Ferryman obviously thought the better of complaining. I was Spike's only hope.

We left her cabin and she marched down to the Shopping Arcade.

"There," she said, pointing at Diandra, who'd been protesting at the Purser's Desk earlier. "That one. Do you suspect her?"

"I suspect everyone," I said.

"Fuck that dog," Kevin Blaney said, in his office on Aloha Deck. His walls were covered with pictures of submarines and fighter jets. He had a photo on his desk of a dozen men in scuba gear and wetsuits, arranged in two rows, their faces deliberately obscured by masks and mouthpieces.

"I thought perhaps he'd fallen overboard, and suggested it to Miss Ferryman, but she was adamant he hadn't."

"He hasn't fallen overboard," Kev confirmed.

"You know that for a fact, do you? Have you checked the CCTVs?"

The *Sapphire* didn't have much by way of high-tech security. There were a couple of cams installed on the Promenade Deck but that was about it.

"Trust me, Jason."

"Can I look at the footage?"

"No."

"Do you know where he is?"

"No."

"It's a small ship. Not a lot of places to hide a yappy Chihuahua. Is he still alive?"

"Stay out of it, Jason. For your own well-being. And the dog's."

I was pretty certain Kevin knew what had happened to Lord Fothergill. And was probably protecting whoever had taken him. But I didn't want to end up bundled into a rope locker, my desperate cries for help ignored until we docked in Juneau. Spike was still with us and that's all I needed to know.

———◆———

They sold everything in the Shopping Arcade, from fleece jackets embossed with StarSea's logo to "personal convenience" items, to high end cosmetics and, of course, jewellery and ceramic figurines. I did a circuit of the Tanzanite counter where Diandra had been accosted by Spike the night before.

Diandra was not the jewellery specialist. Her post was on the other side of the foyer, where they sold toothpaste and Aspirin. And that's where I found her, arguing with Danny, who was attempting to buy seasick tablets. She appeared to be trying to prevent it.

She lost the argument. Danny signed for the tablets and stormed out of the Arcade.

"Lover's tiff?" I inquired, boldly, presenting her with a tube of Colgate for Sensitive Teeth.

"I told him to visit the Crew Doctor but he won't listen to me. He hates doctors."

"Very foolish of him," I agreed. I wanted her on my side. "I saw you at the Purser's Desk this morning complaining about Lord Fothergill."

"Who?"

"Spike. The Chihuahua."

"Ah. Yes. The one that's now gone missing," Diandra confirmed, popping my toothpaste into a little StarSea bag and presenting the chit for my signature.

"So—you know about that..."

"Word travels fast."

"Did Spike frighten you?"

"Me? No." She pooh-poohed the very idea. "I love animals. All of them. I was a certified dog-walker before I joined the *Sapphire*. I had to do a course."

"Then why were you complaining at the Purser's Desk?"

Diandra looked at me. "Danny made me do it. He wanted to make a point."

"I understand you were in the vicinity of the Enclosed Prom this morning when Spike disappeared. About 10 a.m."

Diandra looked uncomfortable. "Who said that?"

"You were seen."

"Please don't tell The Dragon Lady."

"I won't mention that you'd stepped away from your post if you tell me what you were doing standing in that doorway."

"One of the passengers forgot his phone and I was trying to see if I could find him to give it back."

"Why not just keep it safe and wait for him to retrace his steps?"

"I don't know," Diandra said. "I thought I could catch him."

"And did you?"

"No. Unfortunately."

"Did you happen to notice Miss Ferryman and Lord Fothergill?"

Diandra thought for a moment. "No."

"Do you have any thoughts about who might have been annoyed enough at the dog to kidnap him?"

Diandra paused. "Ask Danny," she said, handing me the little StarSea bag.

Danny was arranging photos from the Welcome Aboard dinner on the display racks at the Photo Gallery across from the Atrium Room.

"How are you feeling?" I asked, stopping in front of an 8 x 10 of Honey and Mitch, in their matching turquoise windbreakers, toasting the camera with glasses of wine in one hand and cellphones with pictures of their glasses of wine in the other.

"Better," Danny said. "Thanks."

Some people suffer terribly from motion sickness—my sister is one of them. She can't read in cars or on buses, and if you put her on the water in any kind of conveyance, even if it's calm, you're asking for trouble. Some people are only affected by rougher seas. And some people, like me, seem to be immune to everything. Danny was like my sister. I could have suggested half a dozen other occupations that he'd have been more suited for, on land, but there's no accounting for the spirit of adventure.

"I'm looking into the disappearance of Miss Ferryman's Chihuahua."

"Good riddance, as far as I'm concerned," Danny replied. "He ruined an expensive pair of shoes. Brand new, too."

"I understand you were taking Miss Ferryman's picture this morning roundabout the time the dog disappeared."

"I was taking a lot of pictures of a lot of passengers. It's my job."

"Yes but you provided enough of a distraction that she didn't notice when she became separated from Lord Fothergill."

"And you think I did that deliberately?"

"It had crossed my mind. And your purchase of seasick tablets just now wouldn't have anything to do with possibly keeping Lord Fothergill sedated and quiet for the duration of this cruise...?"

"Very definitely not," said Danny. "I had nothing to do with that damned dog's disappearance. In spite of what Diandra might have told you."

"Why would she implicate you?"

"I've got no idea," Danny said, as Mitch and Honey approached him, cellphones out. "But if you're looking for someone who really hates dogs, check out the ship's *maître d'*."

I knew Marcello would be busy dealing with lunch. So I went upstairs to Lido and the Outside Prom, where the bottoms of our lifeboats hung overhead and, if you looked down the length of the ship, you were reminded of her past glories as a passenger liner, and not of her current itinerary, cruising in endless circles.

And that was where I spotted it.

A feather.

The feather.

A little worse for wear, having been blown by the wind into a corner occupied by one of the tall wooden lockers that contained our spare lifejackets. But it was purple. And it was Spike's.

And it was on the deck above the deck where he'd last been seen.

If I'd been a forensics expert I'd have bagged it immediately and subjected it to a microscopic examination. Lacking a bag and anything remotely resembling a lab, I picked it up and took it up one more flight of stairs to the Sports Deck, which featured a netted basketball court and tables and chairs at the aft end, and the TopDeck Lounge overlooking the bow. In between was a hinterland off-limits to passengers. This was where the crew would go to swing the davits out to launch the lifeboats if it became necessary to abandon ship. The *Sapphire,* of course, would be dead in the water if that ever happened. Her engines would be off, her massive twin screws stopped. Here and now, while we were underway and sailing at about 20 knots through the Inside Passage, it was windy and noisy—I was up beside the ventilation shafts and our immense navy blue funnel.

Again, I wasn't sure what I was looking for. A place in which to hide an annoying Chihuahua? I glanced at the lifeboats, which were mostly the old-fashioned open kind, with a deep hull and a capacity for about 100 occupants squeezed in shoulder-to-shoulder on narrow benches. The *Sapphire* had eight of those—covered over with orange tarps—and another four completely enclosed tenders, for puttering back and forth, ship to shore, when we were anchored in shallow waters. There were also seventy-four inflatables, stacked in various places on the outside decks in white fibreglass barrels.

Even if I'd thought one of the lifeboats would be a logical place to hide a kidnapped dog, I couldn't actually do anything to try and confirm my suspicions. It was too noisy to hear anything except the roar from the funnel and the rush of the wind. And I couldn't easily reach the boats—it would have involved a good deal of clambering and manipulation of mechanisms—something that clearly wasn't detailed in my talent contract (except in dire emergencies).

I debated whether Spike's disappearance might be considered just such an emergency, and came to the conclusion that it wouldn't.

Popping the feather into my jacket pocket, I went back down to the Enclosed Prom, the last place Miss Ferryman had been with Lord Fothergill. I wasn't sure what I was looking for. Stray Chihuahua hairs? Random scatological deposits...?

There's an edict all StarSea employees must follow. It's posted in the crew stairways and lifts. We're required to Smile and Always Greet Guests in a Friendly Manner. I did so as I strolled past the steamer chairs and the little gatherings of passengers, intent on trying to spot bears and whales as we cruised past colourful fishing boats and pristine harbours. I even smiled at a visually impaired guest with his seeing-eye dog.

Miss Ferryman was in the Atrium Room, keeping company with an assortment of *petit fours*.

"I need to ask you something," I said.

Miss Ferryman didn't offer me any of her pastries.

"When you saw the shoppie standing in the doorway...was it open or shut?"

"Why do you ask?"

"Just curious."

"It was open. Wide open."

"But the shoppie definitely wasn't holding it that way."

"Not at all," said Miss Ferryman. "And I don't see what that has to do with anything."

———— ◦ ————

The door in question was always kept shut while we were underway in order to maintain the ship's climate control. Diandra must have propped it open in order to be standing in the position Miss Ferryman had described. I squatted down at Spike-level, and looked around. It was a busy thoroughfare, containing the Shopping Arcade, the Photo Gallery, Ladies and Gents public toilets, a main staircase and two passenger lifts. If Diandra *had* lured Spike away, she would have very quickly had to conceal him somewhere out of sight.

I stood up again and walked across to the Ladies' loo. I listened at the door, then knocked, and waited. Nobody there. I slipped inside and did a quick recon of the two stalls and the sink. The bin that contained used paper towels hadn't been emptied since last night. I did a quick check, just in case. No limp Chihuahuas.

Relieved, I left and walked over to the Gents on the other side of the foyer.

Again, the cleaners hadn't been 'round yet. Because if they had, they'd have noticed the little glass dish on the floor under the sink. I recognized it as belonging to the Crew Bar. Slightly chipped and with a well-worn StarSea logo in white on its side. And containing the remnants of something dark brown and strongly smelling of malt...Guinness.

I found Javier near the Aft Prom hot tub, collecting empty plastic drink tumblers to take back to the Pool Bar.

"How's business?" I asked. "Looking forward to your disembarkation?"

"Is busy business," Javier replied, wearily. "You want drink? I can get you."

"Thank you," I said. "Just a fizzy water, please. With a twist of lime."

He went to fetch it while I sat at a little white plastic table beside the deserted outdoor pool. The Alaska run's not like the Caribbean. It's rarely hot, even at the height of summer. It's breezy and cool and most passengers prefer being boiled alive in the jacuzzi to the temperate chill of the swimming pool.

"You've heard about the disappearance of Lord Fothergill," I checked, when Javier returned with my drink.

"The dog."

"Yes, the dog. The one who made a mess beside the hot tub last night. You had to clear it up."

"Is my job," Javier shrugged.

"Yet you were at the Purser's Desk this morning to lodge a complaint."

"Was there because Chief Pool Butler say, come with me, we make voice together."

"So you were only there because Peter encouraged you. And you felt nothing bad about the dog?"

"I think about getting off ship and flying home. No think about bad stinking dog."

"I saw you in the TopDeck Lounge last night, buying some Guinness."

"So what? Was late. Nobody there, everyone in bed. Just you playing with yourself. Nobody to complain about deck steward out of uniform in off-limits passenger bar."

"What did you do with the Guinness?"

"Took to cabin. Save for later."

I didn't believe him. You can tell when some people aren't telling the truth, and Javier was like a big see-through picture window. But I didn't have a chance to ask him anything else because his presence was required at another table for drink orders, and our guests always took priority.

I collected my fizzy water and went over to Jackson, the drink-slinger behind the Pool Bar.

"You've been on duty since your shift began?" I asked.

"Since 9.00am," Jackson replied. "And I had nothing to do with that dog's disappearance."

I laughed. The entire ship had to know about Spike by now—and about me being asked to investigate.

"Can you just tell me if Javier was here at about 10am?"

"He was," Jackson confirmed.

"And he didn't leave at all?"

"He's been working solidly for the past couple of hours."

"No pee breaks, nothing."

"Two pee breaks—and he used that one." He nodded at the Gents loo behind the bar.

"Not the toilet near the Shopping Arcade?"

"Of course not," Jackson said, as if I was daft.

It was time to consult the Captain's Secretary.

Sal's office was tucked in behind the Bridge. It was a storage-cup-board-sized cubby-hole housing the usual business furniture. Sal, who was my age, had made a career out of sailing the seas. She had long dark hair tied back with a big black bow. She was considered an officer—she had tabs on her shoulders—and the ribbon wasn't regulation, but the Captain liked her and nobody dared make an issue of it. On that after-noon, she was sorting through the week's start-of-cruise paperwork.

"Let me guess," she said. "You're hot on the trail of the missing Chi-huahua. I was just processing the documents for USPH. We actually have two support dogs on board this week." She flipped the report around, so that I could have a quick look. "Mr. Chandler. And Ambrose. Quite an interesting story there."

I read the comments from Barrie and Quentin about the fellow with the guide dog I'd encountered during my tour of the Enclosed Prom. Interesting indeed.

"How can I help you with Lord Fothergill?" Sal inquired.

"Do you know who snatched him?"

"Absolutely not."

I believed her. She was—and still is—one of the most honest people I've ever met.

"Unless you've made it your business not to know," I said, after a moment. "Someone mentioned to me that Marcello hates dogs. Might you be able to comment on that? Or anyone else...?"

Sal didn't say anything. She got up and opened the middle drawer in the filing cabinet.

And then had second thoughts as the ship's First Officer appeared in the doorway with a request for her to please join the Captain on the Bridge.

"Crew dockets are confidential," she reminded me, over her shoulder, as she followed him out.

Afterwards, I reclaimed my steamer chair on Aft Prom. And it was while I was there, keying my thoughts into my phone—along with a group invitation to all my suspects to join me in the *Sapphire's* library at half-past two—that I was visited by Mr. Chandler. And Ambrose.

"Good afternoon," he said.

"'Afternoon," I replied, with my required smile.

"I understand you're looking into the disappearance of a dog."

"The entire ship must know about it by now."

"And most of the internet," Mr. Chandler said, amused. He commandeered an empty chair beside me. "Mind if I join you? It's just that I think I might have some information you might find useful."

I knew we'd be undisturbed in the *Sapphire's* library. Even though it featured computers as well as books in glass-fronted cabinets, comfy armchairs and writing tables, it was one of the least-used places aboard the ship.

I waited for everyone to arrive, and then posted a little sign that said PRIVATE MEETING on the door, and closed it.

There they were: my rogues' gallery. Diandra the shoppie and Danny the photographer. The Seawind's *maître d'*, Marcello. Chief Purser Barrie and Quentin, his assistant. Samuel, the TopDeck's bartender and Carla, the waitress, and Javier the Deck Steward and Peter the Chief Pool Butler. Chef Franco, with his legendary short fuse.

And Mr. Bothwell, the passenger with the phobia of dogs.

"Are we expecting ruff seas?" Quentin inquired.

"Murder on the Ketchikan Express?" Samuel quipped.

I smiled.

"You may all be wondering why I've assembled you here," I said. "I believe that you may all have some information which will help me solve Lord Fothergill's disappearance."

My guests looked confused.

"Diandra," I said. "I know you were not actually in your shop at 10.00 a.m.. In fact, you were in the foyer near the Promenade door."

"That's right. Yes."

"You told me that you didn't recall seeing Miss Ferryman and Lord Fothergill. But I don't believe you. You couldn't have avoided seeing them. As well as Danny. Would you like to change your statement?"

Diandra looked conflicted.

"Yes," she admitted, finally. "OK. I saw them."

"And what were they doing?"

"Miss Ferryman was having words with Danny. He was trying to take her picture."

"And Miss Ferryman was reluctant to allow him to do so."

"Yes. That's a good way to describe it."

"And while she was preoccupied with Danny...what was happening with Lord Fothergill?"

"I already told you...I have no idea."

"In fact," I said, "I believe he was investigating the door, which you'd propped open. Am I correct?"

Diandra hesitated. "Yes."

"And do you happen to know why Lord Fothergill was so interested in this propped-open door?"

"Because I offered him a treat. I felt sorry for him! It's ridiculous the way that woman dresses him up in silly clothes. What about his dignity? I just wanted to tell him that I understood how he must have felt and I wanted to show him a little compassion. I didn't mean any harm."

"And then what happened?"

"He ran off."

"In which direction?"

"Towards the Gentlemen's toilets."

"And you didn't think to stop him or go after him?"

"I was...distracted."

"By what?"

Diandra looked at Danny. And then: "Not by what. By who. By Marcello."

"And what was Marcello doing to distract you?"

"He was..." She looked down. "Kissing me."

"And was this display of public affection welcomed?"

Diandra paused, and then nodded. "But it wouldn't have been welcomed if you hadn't started secretly dating Carla behind my back," she said, to Danny.

"You drove me to it!" Danny objected. "Always going on about my dream of setting up a studio specializing in dog and cat portraits."

"Dogs and cats dressed in stupid outfits in ridiculous poses."

"No worse than wrapping newborns up like Egyptian mummies and pretending they're bumble bees and flower buds—which is what you seem to be obsessed with these days!"

"Let me just clear something up," I interrupted. "Why were you buying seasickness tablets in the shop this morning?"

"I have gastric reflux. That dog aggravated my condition. And I was all out of prescription meds."

"So it wasn't for seasickness at all."

"No. The stuff I was buying is 100% ginger."

"Not the stuff that has Dimenhydrinate in it."

"That only works for nausea and vomiting. Not for what's wrong with me."

"So if you'd wanted to drug Lord Fothergill...it would have been completely ineffective."

"Completely," said Danny, glaring at Diandra.

"Thank you."

I turned my attention to Marcello. "I happen to know that you dislike dogs."

"Many people do," Marcello answered, diplomatically. "Do you suspect me of an impropriety?"

"Did you abduct Lord Fothergill?"

"No," said Marcello. "I would rather leave it to someone else."

There was laughter in the ship's library.

"Exactly my point," I said. "Can it be that your kissing Diandra was another distraction, to allow someone else the opportunity to do the deed?"

Marcello didn't say anything.

"In fact," I said, "you've requested that you be exempted from duty whenever service dogs are in the dining room. You shouldn't even have been there last night. But the crewmember who should have replaced you was in bed with gastroenteritis. When you were a very young boy, you were given a little puppy, which you adored more than anything else in the world. But you let it out of your sight and it was trodden on by your careless uncle and was killed. The trauma has affected you ever since. Am I right?"

"Yes," Marcello admitted. "I rarely speak of it."

"Who asked you to distract Diandra?"

"I dare not say."

"Someone who carries some weight aboard this ship," I guessed.

"Certainly not me," Barrie said. "I have a wonderful dog at home, a border collie named Lad. I wish that bloody Lord Fothergill had never come aboard—but I also didn't have anything to do with his disappearance."

"I know you didn't," I said.

"And I hope you don't suspect me either," said Quentin.

"I don't," I said. "I know you'd never risk your position in the Purser's Office over a contemptuous Chihuahua."

I turned to Javier.

"As for you, Javier...you don't drink. You attend the crew meetings of Friends of Bill W and Dr. Bob. Why were you buying Guinness last night? Have you fallen off the wagon?"

Javier looked annoyed. But he was leaving the ship in Juneau and I reckoned I could risk exposing his secret.

Peter, the Head Pool Butler, raised his hand. "He was getting the Guinness for me."

I looked at him. "Why would he need to do that when you can get it yourself from the Crew Bar?"

"They'd run out."

"I can check that, you know."

"Then do. You'll see I'm telling the truth. I felt like some Guinness and sent Javier to find it. Samuel was very accommodating."

I looked at Samuel. "I do believe you were more than accommodating on this occasion. You also threw in a bottle of Blue Curacao."

Samuel smiled, but didn't say anything.

"I wonder," I said, "who else aboard this ship has a fondness for Blue Curacao?"

I looked at Samuel and Peter and Javier. And then at Carla, who glanced at Chef Franco.

"Ah," I said. "Chef Franco. Whose wife has recently left him for a man who breeds Chihuahuas, and who has been on report more than once since joining the ship for staying in bed and nursing a hangover instead of going to work."

Chef Franco also chose not to reply.

I turned my attention to Mr. Bothwell, who was sitting beside a table which contained a partially-completed jigsaw puzzle.

"You have a phobia of dogs, do you not, Mr. Bothwell?"

"I do."

"I'm sure you had motive and opportunity. But not, alas, the where-withal. It's difficult to stow a Chihuahua in a passenger cabin. Your steward would have discovered it very quickly...unless of course...you have him stuffed in the safe."

Diandra gasped. "He'd be dead in minutes!"

"I did not kidnap that dog and stuff it into my safe," Mr. Bothwell said, indignantly. "You're very welcome to go and look."

"That won't be necessary. Do you know where the root of your fear of dogs lies?"

"When I was a newborn I was nearly smothered by a Chihuahua," Mr. Bothwell replied. "I blame my mother for leaving me unattended on the changing table. I'm working with my therapist to recover these hidden, dark memories."

"And your mother, Mr. Bothwell, is...?"

"The wife of Chef Franco," Mr. Bothwell said, after a moment.

"Soon-to-be-former-wife," Chef Franco corrected, spitefully. "Mr. Bothwell, he is my step-son."

"I can confirm that," said Barrie. "He's aboard the ship as a guest of our Executive Chef."

"And you both despise Chihuahuas...as well as Mrs. Franco. So it would not," I said, "be a stretch to suggest that it was Chef Franco who encouraged Marcello to distract Diandra, giving Mr. Bothwell an opportunity to lure Lord Fothergill into the Gentlemen's toilets. Where you, Chef Franco, were waiting to ensure he would cause no more disruptions aboard this ship."

"You can prove nothing," Chef Franco declared, standing up.

"Sit down," I said. "I believe I can."

I got up and opened the Library door.

"Please come in," I said, to Mr. Chandler and Ambrose.

They entered and I led them to a seat as far away from Mr. Bothwell as possible.

"I just want to say that you're not in any trouble, Mr. Chandler. "Were you in the gentlemen's toilet near the Atrium Room at about 10.00 this morning?"

"I was," Mr. Chandler confirmed.

"And do you recall if there was anyone else in there with you?"

"There was."

"Can you identify that person in this room?"

Mr. Chandler turned his head towards Chef Franco. "Him."

"Impossible," Chef Franco declared. "This man cannot see!"

"In fact," I said, "Mr. Chandler can see perfectly well. It's his dog, Ambrose, who has lost his sight. He was questioned last night after he was spotted by one of the ship's officers, leading Ambrose to the sandbox so that he could relieve himself."

"I couldn't leave him at home," Mr. Chandler explained, removing his sunglasses. "He's been with me for fifteen years and he doesn't have much time left. I thought I could just tell a little fib...he is an Assistance Dog. But I'm the one providing the assistance."

"And can you tell me what you saw in the gentlemen's toilet?" I inquired.

"I saw the little dog with the purple feather, and I saw that man there. And that man there had a bowl filled with something...if I didn't know better I'd have said it was beer...dark beer..."

"Guinness?" I suggested.

"It may have been Guinness."

"Chihuahuas love Guinness," said Diandra.

"Could the Guinness have been used to sedate Lord Fothergill?" I asked.

"I believe so," Diandra said. "Yes."

"Did you see what happened next?" I asked Mr. Chandler.

"I didn't. Ambrose and I left. But that man..." He nodded at Chef Franco. "...had a large shopping bag with him."

"I suggest," I said, to Chef Franco, "that after you administered the Guinness to Lord Fothergill, you waited in a cubicle until it took effect, after which you popped Lord Fothergill into your shopping bag and spirited him away. Where is he, Chef Franco?"

Chef Franco glared at Mr. Chandler, and then at me, and then at Ambrose. And then he leaped up and made a calculated run for it, sprinting past the sightless dog, yanking the library door open and disappearing down the passenger stairs before I could stop him.

He wasn't going to get far. He obviously couldn't get off the ship. I followed him down, knowing he was running on adrenaline, from the Sports Deck, to Lido, Promenade, Aloha and Baja. That was where he tried to lose me, ducking down narrow corridors that led through the labyrinth of passenger cabins. He didn't count on me knowing more about the *Sapphire's* layout than he did. But he'd only been on the ship for three weeks; I'd been aboard for the whole season.

I was waiting for him by the portside door to the Showcase Lounge—really the only place he could end up, given his trajectory.

All the new ships have their entertainment venues purpose-built. Lovely huge rooms that can accommodate everything from circus acts to water ballets to stage shows direct from Las Vegas. Our little Showcase Lounge was tiny, created out of the ship's original cinema. It had storage space underneath its stage for costumes and props and which, I could confidently state, now secreted a very vocal Chihuahua who, from the aroma surrounding the general area, was also suffering from a very messy case of Guinness-induced diarrhea.

"Are you going to liberate the poor thing," I said, to Chef Franco, "or shall I?"

"Take him," Chef Franco said, spitefully, yanking Spike out of his cubbyhole prison and pitching him at me.

I caught him before he could crash to the floor.

With an ungrateful snarl, Spike sank his teeth into my arm.

"*I hate you*," I said, disengaging his mouth and holding his snout closed with my free hand so he couldn't inflict any more damage to my anatomy. "You're lucky a Cocker Spaniel saved me from drowning at the seaside when I was ten. Otherwise, right now, you'd very definitely be sleeping with the Orcas."

If Miss Ferryman was at all grateful for Lord Fothergill's return, she had an odd way of letting me know.

"Where is his cardigan?" she demanded, as I handed him over. I'd given him a quick rinse in my cabin, lathered him with my favourite lemon and lime shower gel and fluffed him up with my hairdryer. "And his scarf? And his *feather*?"

"I'm afraid I have no idea," I replied. The scarf and the cardigan had been discretely discarded in triple-wrapped rubbish bags. There was no way I was giving back the feather.

"We are disembarking in Juneau," Miss Ferryman said, full of spite. "And your Head Office will be hearing from us."

"I'm sorry you feel that way," I said, dismissing her with my best StarSea Customer Service Training Manual smile.

I waited until we'd sailed out of Juneau before I stuck Spike's purple feather in the fretboard of my favourite acoustic guitar, up between the nut and the tuning pegs, where smokers usually jam their ciggies.

"I'd like to dedicate my first song tonight," I said, as my audience trickled in, "to a memorable little fellow who brought us all a little closer together this week."

I really needed a banjo and a mandolin and an upright bass to do the tune justice. It was Bluegrass, in the truest sense of the word. But I'd laid down some backing tracks on my magic machine, and I could handle the accompaniment with just my Gibson.

"For Spike," I said, to a smattering of appreciative laughter. "'Salty Dog Blues'."

ABOUT SALTY DOG BLUES...

This is a very long short story, or a very short novella, depending on your point of view.

"Salty Dog Blues" was written in 2019, following publication of my second Jason Davey mystery, *Notes on a Missing G-String*, and was included in the anthology *Crime Wave*, published by Sisters in Crime—Canada West in November 2020.

Eight years earlier, Jason Davey, the story's sleuth, had made his debut in a standalone novel, *Cold Play* (2012), working as an entertainer on board an Alaska-bound cruise ship.

In "Salty Dog Blues", I took Jason back to his nautical roots, and gave him a very tongue-in-cheek mystery to solve.

A second character, Abigail Ferryman, also owes her legacy to *Cold Play*. In the novel, an aging actress, Diana Wyndham, comes aboard the *Star Sapphire* to make life difficult for Jason. In the story's earlier drafts, one of Diana's myriad complaints was an allergy to the colour blue. I couldn't quite make it work in later drafts and so, reluctantly, those scenes were cut.

But they weren't lost forever—I resurrected them for Abigail Ferryman, whose character perfectly lent itself to just such a difficulty.

Chronologically, the story takes place a few weeks prior to *Cold Play* in the summer of 2012.

"Salty Dog Blues" was a finalist in the Crime Writers of Canada's 2021 Awards of Excellence for Best Crime Novella.

10

BLUE DEVIL BLUES

"Can you sing?" the man asked.

His name was Howard Parfitt and he was wearing a wig. Not a toupee or a topper. A full wig—the sort of thing older men put on their heads when the Beatles were just starting to make it big in the early 1960s and they wanted to be "with it" and "trendy" but they didn't have enough hair of their own to pull off the classic mop top with a fringe.

It was a black wig. It made him look ridiculous, quite frankly, but it was his club—Diamonds—and Diamonds featured vintage rock and roll, with a special emphasis on the Swinging Sixties, and he was legendary for looking the part.

Howard Parfitt was about 70 years old and he'd been running Diamonds since 1990, when he'd taken it over from his dad. Peter Parfitt had opened the club in 1965, a rock and roll mecca in the heart of London's Soho, three minutes from Carnaby Street and *the* place to mingle (if you could get in) for any number of years.

Those heady days were long gone, however. And Diamonds was struggling. I knew it was struggling when I turned up for the audition. I was struggling too. It was 2016 and I'd come back to England after a couple of years abroad and I needed the work. I'd done the rounds. I'd approached managers and agents and record producers and the owners of other clubs. I'd even resorted to busking. I was losing faith in my talent and I was scared to death I was going to end up a sad guitar-player in a tunnel somewhere, playing "Smoke on the Water" for spare change.

This was my very last shot.

"I can sing," I confirmed.

Howard Parfitt sat back in his chair and waited.

I'd brought along three of my mates who were also musicians. Like Harry in "Sultans of Swing" (and unlike me) they had daytime jobs and they were doing all right.

They usually played jazz.

I usually played jazz.

We'd run through our collection of rock and roll instrumentals. "FBI"—made famous by The Shadows, but I preferred a lesser-known arrangement by The Apaches—it rocks and has lots of cheeky key changes; "Short Trip", by Little Louie, from 1964—which nobody's ever heard of except me; "Hall of the Mountain King"—a sax-drenched favourite, a classic by Grieg made famous by Sounds Incorporated, who used to open for The Beatles when they went on tour; "Side Winder"—the signature tune of a Canadian band, Wes Dakus and The Rebels, which was Keith Hampshire's theme when he was a DJ aboard the pirate ship Radio Caroline; and "Because They're Young", the Duane Eddy hit I've always really loved because of its solid twangy lead guitar and its full orchestra backing—which Dave emulated magnificently on his portable keyboard.

"Please," said Howard Parfitt, gesturing with his hands. "Sing."

We'd considered the possibility that this might happen and, fortunately, we'd rehearsed a party piece. Rudy, Ken and Dave played me in and I launched into my absolutely stonking rendition of "Fireball XL5".

Howard Parfitt burst into delighted laughter.

Fireball XL5 was a Gerry and Sylvia Anderson-produced Supermarionation kids' show that aired on British tv in the early 1960s. I shared Neil Gaiman's fond recollection of a childhood informed by "bad puppet science fiction." And I loved its closing theme, which was sung by Don Spencer, an Australian who'd gone on to accomplish great things in children's television and whose daughter had grown up to marry Russell Crowe.

"Thank you," Howard said, still grinning, as we finished. "You're not very good, are you?"

This, coming from a 70-year-old man wearing a black Beatle wig, an egg-stained blue paisley tie and scuffed brown suede boots with Cuban heels and pointy toes that my mum used to refer to as "winkle pickers."

He was shortly going to turn up dead—still wearing his wig, the winkle pickers and his blue paisley tie. But of course, I had no inkling about that.

I glanced doubtfully at Ken, Rudy and Dave.

"I mean," Howard said, looking at me, "you're good."

Then he nodded at my band.

"You aren't."

"They are good," I objected, "but they'd really rather be playing jazz."

"Not my thing, unfortunately," Howard replied. "My brother Harry's quite a fan though."

If I'd known then what I found out later, I'd have warned him about his brother's branch of the family. But, hindsight.

"Does Harry have a nightclub?" Ken asked.

Howard laughed again. "Sorry. No. He's my accountant."

"Could we play some jazz for you?" Dave tried.

Howard checked his watch.

"Oh all right. Go on, then."

We did an old standard from 1929, "Blue Devil Blues". As originally written it's in C minor and has a slow rhythm, but we'd perked it up and given it a catchy beat and whenever we played it (in pubs and the odd club gig) the punters loved it.

I like to think Howard was appreciative. Last impressions and all that.

"Much better," he said, when we were done. "Thanks."

Dave looked happier.

"Anyway—thanks for coming."

And that was that. We unplugged our instruments from the club's sound system. Rudy packed up his drum kit and we helped him carry all his cases out. I remember feeling particularly deflated. I really wasn't looking forward to setting up my pitch in Covent Garden again. You can take in a decent amount of money on a good weekend when there are lots of tourists around and you're playing tunes they recognize. But it's not a steady income and sometimes it rains and I was well past the young and adventurous and living-off-tinned-beans stage in my life.

Another band was waiting in the foyer. They were dressed identically in collarless grey suit jackets and tightly-knotted ties and trousers with drainpipe legs and collectively they looked about 19 years old. I held the door open for them as they trekked into the venue with all their gear.

Rudy, Ken and Dave took their leave, but I decided to stay. I wanted to hear if the Beatle boys were any better than we were.

I sat down in a comfy chair in the foyer to listen to their version of "Love Me Do". Their grandparents hadn't even been born when that song had charted in 1962.

They were in the middle of "I Want to Hold Your Hand" when a woman came into the foyer from the street. She had an old acoustic guitar with her—not in a case—and she was wearing a leather vest with fringes on it, a blue t-shirt that advertised the 2012 London Olympics, a pair of jeans with the knees frayed out and torn and a blue Zorro hat. She had short straight blonde hair. I reckoned she was in her mid-twenties.

"You waiting too?" she asked, sitting in the chair beside me.

"Just finished," I replied. "Don't call us, we'll call you."

"Sounds familiar." She stuck out her hand. "Evie Parfitt."

"Jason Davey," I said. "You related to Howard?"

"His niece," she said. "My dad's Harry Parfitt. The accountant."

"And your uncle's making you audition?"

"Sadly. But he's keen to save me from ending up as a root-less, aimless person with no purpose in life."

I had to admire Howard's sense of fair play. I hate nepotism. I've spent my life consciously trying to avoid it. I was certain if I'd mentioned my musical pedigree and my real name to Howard, he'd have bent over backwards to accommodate me. But that's not how I roll. Or rock.

"Show me your guitar?" Evie asked.

I unlatched my case and let her have a look.

"Very nice," she said. "It looks old. An original?"

"Very much an original," I replied. And I told her about its history. The fact that my dad and mum were the founding members of Figgis Green, a folky pop band who were big in the 1960s and 1970s. My dad, Tony Figgis, had died in 1995 and my mum had given me two of his guitars. One of them— a Sunburst Strat—went to the bottom of the Gulf of Alaska in 2012 when the cruise ship I was working on caught fire and sank. This was the other—a Lake Placid Blue Strat. I was glad I hadn't taken it to sea. I was counting on it to bring me some luck.

"Worth a few bob, I imagine," Evie said.

"I could never sell it."

Evie, in turn, told me her story. All her life she'd wanted to be a singer. But she hadn't been very successful. The Parfitt name had opened doors...but she hadn't managed to make any headway once she'd stepped over the threshold. She'd performed in pubs and clubs, at farmer's markets and store openings. She was passionate about her craft.

She was passionate about the London Underground, too.

"I write all my own songs," she said. "A lot of them are about the tube."

She sang one of them for me, accompanying herself on her old battered acoustic guitar. It was about an out-of-work musician riding around all day on an Underground train.

It wasn't very good.

She sang me a second song. It sort-of reminded me of something from *Starlight Express*. It was about an Under-ground train as well.

And it wasn't very good either.

"You do know that your Uncle Howard's looking for a rock and roll act," I said.

"Of course," Evie replied.

And then she sang "Love of the Loved". The one written by Paul McCartney that Cilla Black recorded for her debut single in 1963. It was dreadful. But at least it wasn't about an Underground train.

The band that was auditioning inside the main venue for Evie's Uncle Howard had fallen silent. They'd been playing "Yellow Submarine." I wondered if they were undergoing an existential crisis and were looking for a handy Maharishi and the opportunity to play on a nearby roof.

And I needed to use the loo.

"Any idea where the Gent's is?" I asked.

"In the cellar," Evie said, nodding at a staircase at the end of the foyer. "Turn right at the bottom."

She was obviously well-acquainted with Uncle Howard's club.

I left my guitar in its case beside my chair and went downstairs in search of the toilets. The cellar wasn't all that inviting. It was dark and it smelled like mildew. There were lit-up emergency Way Out signs, but that was it for the corridor.

And the toilets had seen much better days. Fluorescents flickered in the ceiling and the walls were covered with shiny white fired clay tiles, but a lot of them had been chipped and cracked by the passage of time and many had simply come loose and fallen away.

I relieved myself and went back upstairs. The band still weren't playing—but I could hear them chatting and laughing on the other side of the closed doors. They'd prob-ably got the gig. Bastards.

I didn't see Evie.

She'd disappeared.

And so had my dad's Lake Placid Blue Strat.

I really hoped she'd just popped in to chat with the guys in the Beatle suits. I opened the door. They were lounging around the stage. One of them was smoking, in spite of the signs prohibiting it.

But she was not there.

"Haven't seen her, mate," Ringo said, in answer to my question.

I ran outside but I knew it was hopeless. She had a five-minute head start on me and it was mid-afternoon, it was July, and Soho was teeming with tourists.

To say I was devastated would be an understatement. That was my dad's guitar. He'd loved it and nurtured it and I'd kept it safe all those years since he'd died...and now I'd lost it.

My plummeting mood was replaced by rising anger. I knew who Evie was—she'd given me her name. Howard Parfitt was her uncle.

I ran back to the venue.

"He went that way," Paul said, pointing at a door that I guessed led to backstage storage and dressing rooms.

I wasn't wrong. The main lounge was a bit tatty-looking and in dire need of some renovations. Its backstage area, which the punters never saw, was even worse: a narrow hallway scattered with micro-phone stands and lights and bundled electrical cords, broken chairs and three-legged tables, stuff from behind the bar, cardboard boxes, wooden crates.

I didn't hear any voices and I wasn't sure where Howard had gone, so I went looking for him. I checked all the doors. Storage. Dressing room. Dressing room and storage. Toilet. I was down to the last door on the right. I opened it.

It was another dressing room and the lights were on. It was very small. There was a counter against the wall and above it a big mirror and below it a chair. There were pictures on two of the other walls of some of the big-name British performers who'd played at Diamonds in its hey-day. Adam Faith. Marty Wilde. Tommy Steele.

Howard Parfitt was lying on the floor.

He had a very large knife wound in his chest roundabout where his heart was. Quite a lot of blood had exited his body and pooled on the floor around him.

I rang 999 on my mobile and told them what I was looking at.

They asked me to check if he was breathing.

He wasn't.

They asked me to check his neck for a pulse. I did. Very carefully. Mindful of the need not to interfere with the scene of the crime.

There was no pulse.

I really hoped they weren't going to ask me to start CPR while we waited for the ambulance and the police to arrive. I knew how to do it. I'd done lifesaving training as part of the stuff I needed to know when I was working as an entertainer aboard the *Star Sapphire*. How to launch an inflatable life raft. How to leap off a sinking ship (fold your arms across the front of your lifejacket and hold your nose). How to revive someone who's drowned.

Not stabbed through the heart, though, and missing most of his blood.

"Are you in a safe place?" the woman asked.

It hadn't occurred to me but there was always the possibility that Howard's killer was still in the building. I might have put myself in terrible danger.

I looked up. There was nowhere for anyone to hide in the dressing room. There were no cupboards or concealed spaces.

"I'm in the room with the victim," I said.

"If you wouldn't mind waiting outside," the woman said. "Try not to disturb anything. The police and the ambulance will be there shortly."

I gave my statement to Detective Sgt. Hensler. I told her what I was doing there, took her through the audition and what I'd seen and done afterwards. I told her about the band in the Beatle suits and how they'd stopped playing. I told her the approximate time I went to the loo and what time I came back. And I told her about Evie Parfitt and how she'd disappeared along with my dad's guitar.

I could see the little cogs whirring around. Well, they were whirring around in my head, anyway. Could any of the Beatle boys have done it? Not likely. They were all sitting on the stage when I saw them, and none of them really looked like murderers. Ringo had come back to talk to me while we were waiting for the police. He told me Howard's mobile had rung while they were in the middle of "Yellow Submarine". Howard had taken the call, said a few words, waited for them to finish and had told them to take a quick break. And then he'd excused himself, leaving by way of the service door to the backstage area where I'd found him.

I dutifully told Detective Sgt. Hensler what Ringo had told me, mindful of the fact that in her notes, it would be classed as hearsay. But I thought it might be useful. I was sure she'd be taking statements from John, Paul, George and Ringo next anyway.

"And what about the woman you were talking to?" Detective Sgt. Hensler checked her notes. "Evie Parfitt."

"I was sitting with her the entire time," I said.

"Except when you went to use the toilet."

"Yes."

"And when you came back, she was gone."

"Yes," I said. "Along with my guitar."

"And she didn't make any calls on her mobile while you were sitting with her."

"None at all. The band was playing 'Yellow Submarine'. They stopped. I went to the loo."

Those little cogwheels were whirring again. Howard's mobile had rung, he'd taken the call, and then disappeared into the back of the club. Perhaps the call had nothing to do with his murder. Perhaps Evie was upset that her uncle had forced her to audition. She was familiar with the layout of the club. She knew about the doorways and corridors. Perhaps she had a large knife concealed inside the body of her guitar —although I was certain I'd have heard it rattle when she played her Underground songs for me.

"And did anybody else see you when you went down to the Gent's?" Detective Sgt. Hensler inquired, looking at me very directly.

"No," I said. "Just Evie."

Cogwheels.

"Am I a suspect?" I asked.

"You are not," said Detective Sgt. Hensler. "I haven't cautioned you and you are, at this point, simply assisting us with our inquiries."

She took my name and my address and my mobile number.

"Can I report the theft of my Strat?"

"We're the Murder Investigation Team," Detective Sgt. Hensler replied. "Fill out the online form." She gave me a card for the City of London Police's crime report website.

"Thank you," I said, putting it in my pocket.

"Please don't discuss this matter with any other witness-es," Detective Sgt. Hensler replied, pleasantly. "Goodbye."

I knew the chances of the police finding my dad's guitar were next to none. I had photos of it back at my flat and I knew I could get the serial number from my mum and a list of all the modifications my dad had made to it over the years. I also knew I'd have to fill out the online form, if only to get a report filed so that if the Strat ever did surface, they'd have a record of my claim and proof of ownership.

In the meantime, I had some heavy-duty footwork ahead of me. I needed to visit music shops and haunt the websites that bought and sold used musical instruments.

I reckoned I'd have better luck just trying to find Evie.

Her father, the accountant, was easy to locate. His firm had a website. I rang the number and my call was answered by a very efficient-sounding receptionist named Pamela.

"My name's Jason Davey," I said. "Harry's daughter, Evie, was at an audition today and, sadly, I seem to have written her number down wrong. I was wondering if Harry was there and, if he is, whether I might trouble him for Evie's contact info."

"I'm terribly sorry," Pamela replied, "but he's not. In fact, the police have just been here looking for him. Something dreadful's happened to his brother."

"My timing's not very good, is it?" I said. "I hope Howard's all right."

"No—he isn't," said Pamela, her voice sounding a little shaky, "In fact he's been killed. And Harry had only just talked to him this morning on the phone. They were having an argument."

"Was it about Diamonds?" I asked, pushing my luck.

"I think it was. Harry told me Howard had hung up on him! He was in such a mood!"

"I know the club," I said. "It's been losing money for years."

"You're telling me," Pamela replied. "Harry's been trying to convince his brother to cut his losses and shut it down. But Howard wouldn't. And now look what's happened!"

"Indeed," I said, checking the website to see where HL Parfitt Accounting was located. In Soho, about two minutes away from where I was standing.

Had Harry been motivated by profit and loss and done away with his most troublesome client? The phone call Pamela mentioned was in the morning. Harry could have walked around in the afternoon...called his brother again...

"I don't suppose you have Evie's mobile number handy," I said.

"I'm sorry, I don't. But if you can reach Harry perhaps he can help."

She gave me two numbers. The first was for his mobile— which went straight to messaging. The other was for his land-line at home, which was answered by a woman who sounded much younger than Pamela.

"I'm afraid Harry's not here at the moment," said the woman, whose name, it transpired, was Rosalind. "May I take a message?"

I told her who I was, and that Harry hadn't answered my call and I was actually trying to find Evie.

"I've no idea where Evie is," Rosalind said, the tone in her voice changing to something bordering on frosty. "She doesn't live here and I rarely speak to her."

"You're not her mother," I guessed.

"Harry divorced Evie's mother ten years ago," Rosalind replied. "I have as little to do with them as possible. Quite frankly, Evie can't stand the sight of me. The feeling's entirely mutual."

"I'm sorry to hear that," I said. I was pushing my luck again. "Would you happen to have a number for Evie...?"

"I would not. Try Harry's brother."

"Howard?" I said.

"Yes, Howard. The girl's deluded into thinking she has some sort of musical gift. It's all nonsense, of course. But that foolish man encourages it."

"You know he's dead," I said.

There was silence. Then:

"When did this happen?"

"Today."

There was another long silence.

"I must go," Rosalind said, quickly. "I'm sorry. I must make some calls."

Not, *how do you know this?* Or *how did he die?* Or *where was his body found?* All of the curious questions one might ordinarily think would be forthcoming from a murder victim's sister-in-law.

She didn't wait for me to say goodbye.

If I didn't know better, I'd have thought Rosalind wasn't in the least surprised by my news.

There are a number of ways you can try to find people in the UK. Some of them are free but require a lot of searching. Others require the outlay of money—but they save you the search time.

All I wanted was an address and a phone number.

I started with the obvious—the online BT phonebook. It used to be a great resource but these days a lot of people just don't have landlines anymore or they've opted out of being listed. I had to supply a town, so I guessed Evie was living in London. There weren't that many Parfitts that came back as a result of my search. And none of them were "E". I rang them all anyway, just in case. No luck.

Then I checked Facebook. Sometimes people forget to make their contact info private. Evie wasn't one of them, though she did have a fairly robust presence and a lot of her posts were public. They were mostly showcasing her performances or promoting her upcoming gigs. And celebrating her overriding passion, the London Underground. Specifically, London Underground stations, and even more specifically, London Underground stations which were no longer operational and had been abandoned.

She wasn't a bad prose writer and she definitely had the knack of persuasion. She just couldn't write songs. Or sing.

Her Facebook page made for fascinating reading. But it didn't give me her phone number. Or her email address.

I reluctantly arrived at the conclusion that I was going to have to resort to the outlay of money.

I logged onto 192.com and for £14.99 + VAT I was able to generate a background report for Evie Genevieve Parfitt who, it turned out, shared a flat with three other young ladies in Clapham, across the river in SW4.

I was also able to determine her age (25), her mortality (not dead), whether or not she had ever been insolvent or bankrupt (she hadn't), whether she'd ever been listed as a disqualified company director (she hadn't), if she'd ever had any County Court Judgements against her (she hadn't), whether or not she was a property owner (she wasn't), the identities of the co-occupants of the flat where she was living (particularly helpful), but not, however, her telephone number (particularly unhelpful).

But her address, if it was current, was enough.

There are only two deep-level Underground stations that still have island platforms. One of them is Clapham North. The other is Clapham Common. The platform in question is only about 12 feet wide, and it's a truly frightening place at 5pm in the middle of rush hour.

I was in the last carriage of the southbound train, so when I got off I had to trek down the length of the narrow little platform to reach the stairs at the opposite end. It seemed like I was in the company of the entire population of Clapham. And my claustrophobia wasn't helped by the simultaneous arrival of two more trains—one in each direction—accompanied by a hurricane wind that threatened to blast all of us directly into their paths.

Perhaps Evie would have appreciated it for what it was— an original museum piece of Underground railway design, dating from the earliest years of the 20th century. All I could think of was how quickly I could get out of there.

Once I was up on the surface and my racing heart calmed, I found Evie's road and then the building where her flat was. It appeared to be the top floor of a red brick period conversion, one in a row of late-Victorian terraced houses. I rang the bell, and it was answered (I assumed) by one of the three ladies listed in my background report.

I wasn't sure if it was Evie. And I didn't want her bolting down the back stairs and disappearing into the night with my dad's Strat.

"Meals in a Minute," I said, into the intercom. "Delivery for Evie Parfitt."

"She's not here," said the voice.

"Well she's ordered a Curry with Naan and extra Mango Chutney," I said, "and I'm owed 32 quid."

"She's not here," the voice said again. "And she hasn't been here since this morning."

I repeated the address.

"That's right. But there must be some mistake. Ring her up and sort it out."

"Have you got her number?" I said.

The voice on the other end of the intercom gave it to me, without hesitation.

"Thanks," I said. "Have a good evening."

"Yeah, you too."

I dialled her number as I was walking back to Clapham Common. She let it ring a long time before she answered.

"Evie," I said.

She could see who I was on her phone. I don't shield my ID.

"I'm so sorry," she said. "I was going to call you."

"Were you," I said, unimpressed. "Before or after you sold my Strat?"

"I had to get away. Quickly."

"Just give me back my guitar," I said, "and I won't involve the police."

"Please believe me, Jason. Can we meet?"

She sounded desperate.

"Where?" I said.

"Do you know where Romilly Square is?"

I had to think. "Near Cambridge Circus."

"That's it. Number 84. Half an hour?"

"84 Romilly Square," I repeated, keying it into my phone so I could look it up on the map.

Number 84 Romilly Square was up where Charing Cross Road intersected with Shaftesbury Avenue in a giant X in the heart of London's West End.

The building itself was two storeys high and clad entirely in dark red glazed tiles. The top floor had a flat roof and a row of three large arched windows. I could see that the bottom floor, at street level, used to have three large openings. But the one on the left had been completely bricked in.

The opening on the right led to a construction site: scaffolding and mud and bricks bordering on a tiny park with grass and shrubs.

The opening in the middle was occupied by a shop selling used books.

I stood on the pavement looking for Evie, mostly believing that she wasn't going to turn up.

I was wrong.

She appeared from the opening on the right, still wearing her fringed leather vest, her London Olympics t-shirt and jeans. She'd taken off the blue Zorro hat. And her clothes weren't covered in blood, which was a great relief.

"Where's my guitar?" I said.

"Back there," she said, gesturing towards the rear of the red-tiled building.

I followed her through the roofed passageway and she pulled open a grey metal door.

"It's downstairs," she said.

"I'll wait here," I replied. "You can bring it up to me."

"It's 122 steps," she said. She looked around nervously. "And your guitar's really heavy."

"You should have thought of that before you took it," I said.

But she wasn't wrong. Solid body electrics aren't light-weight like wooden acoustics. I reckoned my dad's Strat weighed about nine pounds, and that was without its hard travel case.

"Please come down with me. It's the only place I feel really safe."

It's never a good idea to go into an isolated location with a stranger. Especially someone who might have had something to do with the murder of her uncle. How many victims in horror films have you shouted at for doing just that sort of stupid thing?

But she had my dad's Strat. And I wanted it back.

I followed her inside.

She made sure the door was locked behind me.

"I'll take that," I said, relieving her of the key. "If you don't mind."

She didn't object. Which was reassuring. But only slightly.

We were standing on a concrete platform which had a set of spiral steps leading away from it and down. The platform and the steps were lit by a single functional bulb encased in a steel cage.

"What is this place?" I asked.

"It's an abandoned Underground station," Evie said.

I should have known. "Of course."

She picked up an industrial-sized flashlight from the landing.

"And how did you get the key?" I asked.

"Five years ago they filmed a tv series down here. *Tunnel Land*. One of those weird dark fantasy things. I'm not really a fan, but my boyfriend at the time was working on the production. We used to come back when they weren't filming and explore." She switched on the flashlight. "He's not my boyfriend anymore. But I still have his key."

"After you," I said, following her down the steps, which snaked around a hollow central core. Against the wall I could see white ceramic tiles topped off by repeating green and black lines. There was a handrail, but it didn't look all that reliable.

"These are the old emergency stairs," Evie said, over her shoulder. "They're not in very good shape. Mind how you go."

Going down was going to be a hell of a lot easier than coming back up again, I thought.

"Why was the station abandoned?" I asked.

"That little park outside is right over where the old north-bound platform used to be. It was hit by a stray bomb during the Blitz. The bomb burst through the station tunnel and destroyed the platform and killed 23 people. The line was eventually reopened but the station wasn't. They decided they really didn't need an intermediate stop between Leicester Square and Tottenham Court Road."

"You should go on one of those guided tours where they take people down into the old disused stations and show them all how it used to look."

"I've been on all of them," Evie said. "But this station's never been opened to the public. In fact, it's on a list of buildings shortly to be demolished. It's so sad. It's not even protected. If it was, they wouldn't be able to tear it down." She glanced back at me. "That was another reason why I was waiting to see Uncle Howard this morning. The audition was really just his way of humouring me. I was going to ask him if he could put me in touch with some of his more influential friends. I was trying to think of a way to mount a campaign to save the station. My father and Rosalind have no interest in it at all."

"I spoke to Rosalind," I said, deciding against mentioning Howard's unfortunate death. At least until I'd got my guitar back and I was safely outside again. "I was trying to find you."

"I'm sure she was helpful," Evie said. I noted the sarcasm in her voice. "She can't stand me."

"I did notice."

"I'm not scared of Rosalind but Thomas is insane."

"Thomas...?"

"Her son. He came with the package when my dad got married again." Evie stopped on the stairs. "He has...issues. He's been in and out of prison for violence. Destroying things. Vandalism. Hitting people. He's threatened me—more than once. And he's actually attacked my dad."

She continued down the steps.

"He doesn't know about this place," she added. "It's my refuge."

I think we were probably about three-quarters of the way down when I felt a small breeze and heard a distant rumble. Evie stopped and turned around.

"Stand with your back to it," she said. "And hang onto the handrail."

Common sense told me to take her advice.

The breeze grew into a wind, and the rumble turned into a roar.

"When the trains travel through the tunnels they push the air in front of them like a piston!" Evie shouted.

That had been one of the things which had made the island platform at Clapham Common so terrifying.

As the train hurtled along its tracks in the distance, the piston-wind became a blast that roared through every disused passage and connecting tunnel until it reached the stairs.

"Romilly Square's not a working station anymore so the trains speed through it without slowing down or stopping!" Evie shouted, as the wind pummelled our backs, whipping up 75 years of dust and grime.

I heard the last cars of the train clearing the old station tunnel.

"Turn around now!" Evie advised. "And keep your hand on the railing!"

I hung on as the back-end of the piston sucked the wind out again—this time trying to blow us down the rest of the stairs.

It was over a few seconds later.

"Some refuge," I said.

"You get used to it," Evie replied, shining her torch into the darkness. "This way."

At the bottom of the steps, I followed her into a rounded passage-way lined with the tattered remnants of posters in framed squares. Old ads for Wright's Coal Tar Soap and Oxo cubes and wartime messages from the government: *Careless Talk Costs Lives. Volunteer for Flying Duties. Is Your Journey Really Necessary?*

The rounded passage widened out and I could see two large open-ings in the tiled wall.

"Lift shaft," Evie said. "Those would have been where the doors opened for the two lifts. This side is where the passengers got off after coming down from the surface."

She aimed her light through one of the large openings and I could see a similar opening on the other side of a very large gap.

"They'd go into the lifts on that side for the ride up. There used to be two lifts in here—the old Otis ones that were still being used in 1941. But they took them out. So the lift shaft's empty."

She shone her torch through the nearest opening and I followed her down a short flight of concrete steps into the very bottom of the shaft. She paused and I heard a click, and suddenly, there was light.

I blinked. My eyes had got used to the near-total blackout.

"They never bothered to cut off the electricity after the film crew left. I imagine the lights still work out in the station tunnels as well but I've never been able to find the switches. What do you think?"

What did I think? I was standing at the bottom of an immense cylinder. If I looked up, I could see all the way to the top, where the shaft had been concreted over to form the floor of the bookshop at street level.

And where I was standing had been turned into a kind of rudi-mentary living space. There was a chair, a couple of pillows, two candles. A rug. Some blankets. There was Evie's acoustic guitar, propped against the steps. And there was my guitar case, beside it.

I checked to make sure my dad's Strat was still inside.

"It can get a bit crowded at my flat when all of us are at home at the same time," Evie said. "And it's not a good place to be when Thomas gets into one of his moods and turns up in a rage. This is where I write my songs. This is where I can get some peace and quiet."

The peace and quiet part was debatable.

I heard the dull hum of another train approaching the station. I felt the first stirrings of the wind. I looked for some-thing to hang onto but Evie simply sat down on the floor and suggested that I do the same.

I did.

The wind grew into the familiar roaring hurricane as the piston-driven air flooded into the circular shaft and blew upwards over our heads. The train rattled through the station at full speed, sucking the air behind it, and the hurricane raged again, this time down and out through the four openings, but barely ruffling my hair.

"It's actually very quiet once the trains stop running. That's why they filmed the tv series at night. I find it comforting, really."

It was true. Before the Night Tube service was launched, everything really did shut down at midnight. I also had first-hand knowledge of that—I'd been caught out too many times after I'd missed the last train home.

"Where will you go when they tear down the station?" I asked.

"I don't even want to think about that. It'll be like losing my very best friend in the world."

She looked so unhappy.

I remembered watching the *Tunnel Land* tv series on DVD while I was at sea. I remembered the stunningly peculiar scenes and I remembered wondering if they'd constructed a special set or if the series had been shot on location somewhere.

And now I knew.

I studied the lift shaft's circular wall, and then let my eyes roam up again, to the sealed-off ceiling 80 feet over my head.

"I wonder if my mum might be able to help," I said.

I brought my eyes down to earth again.

"She does know some very influential people. And some of them are quite fond of the Underground."

Evie smiled. "Are you going to turn into my secret angel? I'll have to put you in touch with Uncle Howard."

I had to tell her. I felt awful.

"Evie," I said. "Your Uncle Howard's dead. I'm so sorry."

"No," she said, looking at me. "He can't be...how do you know?"

"I was there," I said, gently. "I found his body. Backstage. Someone stabbed him."

Evie shuddered. "Oh my God," she said. "He was there. Thomas was there. That's why I ran. I saw him. He came out through a door and he saw me. He had that look on his face. I've seen it before. He had a knife...I was so frightened, Jason. I just picked up everything and ran. Including your guitar. He'd have used it to smash something. Me."

"I expect the police have been trying to contact you," I said.

"I was down here. I only went upstairs for something to eat. I didn't check my messages. And then you rang." She looked at me. "Thomas."

"I think you may be right," I said.

"No," said a voice behind me—male. "She means...hello Thomas."

I spun around. He was taller than me—about six foot two, I'd say—and twice as heavy. He looked about Evie's age. He had a shaved head. He was wearing a leather jacket. The jacket was unzipped and I could see dark stains that looked like blood on his t-shirt. He was holding a very large knife.

I glanced back at Evie. She looked terrified.

"I went to your flat," Thomas said. "But of course, you weren't there. And then I saw him." He nodded at me. "He was asking about you. So, I followed him. Heard him say 84 Romilly Square. Got in my car and drove here and parked 'round the corner and waited in that courtyard where all the building's going on. I saw where you came out. And while you were meeting him..." He nodded at me again. "...I opened the door and came downstairs. And here I am."

Neither Evie nor I dared to say anything.

"Surprise," Thomas added.

"Did you kill Howard?" I asked.

"I don't believe I'll give you the satisfaction of answering that," Thomas replied. "I didn't like him. I don't like her, either. And I don't like you. But I do like this place. I think I'll stay after I rid myself of you two."

I could hear the hum of another train approaching.

Thomas took a step forward, waving his knife at Evie and me, slowly, menacingly. He was blocking our escape out of the bottom of the shaft.

I felt the first tiny whispers of the wind and then the hurricane roar as the piston-blast gusted in through the openings, knocking Thomas off balance. Grabbing the neck of my guitar's travel case, I swung with all my might at Thomas's head—and missed.

He was laughing at me as I whirled all the way around and used my momentum to crack the case's body into his knees, sending him crashing to the concrete floor.

"Go!" I shouted to Evie. "Go! Go!"

She raced up the steps ahead of me. I grabbed the flash-light and ran after her as the roar of the passing train faded and the howling wind reversed direction and blew us both into the darkened passage.

Thomas must have got to his feet because I could hear him behind us, swearing. We ran for our lives, through the connecting passage and up the spiral staircase, up and up, my lungs and legs aching. At the top I fumbled for the key, shoved it into Evie's hand and spun around as Thomas lunged at me. I kicked him in the chest as Evie got the door open. He tumbled backwards, crashing head-first down the steps, the knife clattering loose beside him, as we staggered outside.

I thought we were safe—but Thomas's rage had fuelled him and driven his adrenalin and he was behind us again, chasing us through the construction site and the little park and out into the rushing night-time traffic on Shaftesbury Avenue.

I heard him swearing at us as we raced across the road, dodging the cars. I heard the shriek of skidding tires on pavement and then a thud as he was struck by a Lamborghini going well over the speed limit, driven by an 18-year-old with a suspended license.

The impact knocked Thomas out of his shoes.

He crashed head-first into the road ten feet north of us and was dead in seconds.

Evie and I had to give statements to the police. I'd like to say we told the complete truth...but we were economical with some of the details. Not the ones that mattered. Only the ones that would have made little difference to the outcome.

Howard Parfitt's blood matched the blood on Thomas's t-shirt and under his fingernails where he'd been unable to wash it completely away. The police hunted for the murder weapon, and a few days later it was located in the under-growth in the little park behind Number 84 Romilly Square. The only fingerprints on the knife were those belonging to Thomas. Most of Howard's blood had been wiped off, but the forensics people discovered enough to make a definite match.

Howard himself had an amazing send-off...a celebration of life which a huge number of showbiz people attended, well-known and otherwise.

A few months later, I went back to Diamonds to audition with my band. Evie had talked her dad out of closing it down, and Harry had taken over the day-to-day running of the club. Evie'd made a few other suggestions, too—which was why I was there with Rudy, Ken and Dave. And this time, we were playing jazz.

That night, we went back to Romilly Square.

Some further ideas had been floated. Some strings had been pulled. Safety concerns had been met, the electricity had been checked and waivers had been signed. I'd kept my promise to recruit my mum—who, in turn, had contacted a number of her friends. Many of them were the same people who'd been at Howard Parfitt's funeral. And one of them, as luck would have it, was the producer of the *Tunnel Land* series.

It was two o'clock in the morning and the grey metal door at the rear of Number 84 was propped wide open and deco-rated with lights. Signs welcomed everyone to the *SAVE ROMILLY SQUARE FUNDRAIS-ER* and pointed the way in and down. The spiral staircase had been made safe and lit with bright LEDs, as had the passageway that led to the lift shaft.

Inside the lift shaft, seats were set out in rows facing a small makeshift stage we'd erected in front of one of the openings. We'd hung sound baffles on the walls and over-head to improve the acoustics and we'd run cables into the station's electrical supply.

Rudy, Ken, Dave and I took our places, and we played to a packed house.

Evie had asked if she could sing a solo just before the interval but, sadly, her guitar went missing just before she planned to go on.

Our encores were "Last Train Home", the Pat Metheny standard, and "The Train Song" by Acker Bilk.

Evie made a lovely, impassioned speech at the end of the show, detailing the station's history, its importance as a wartime shelter for performers and audiences and its later reincarnation as a set for *Tunnel Land*, which—it transpired— had quite a cult following.

We finished the gig with *Tunnel Land*'s theme song—which wasn't a huge stretch from "Fireball XL5", if I'm honest.

Evie's guitar was eventually found outside in the little park behind the station, very near to where Thomas's knife had been discovered in the bushes. But by then, of course, the show was over and everyone had gone home.

And in the end...

In the end, Romilly Square *was* saved from the wrecker's ball. Tours of its subterranean tunnels were organized to show off *Tunnel Land's* locations, and Evie was hired as a guide. She's still doing it, if you're ever in London and you have a few spare hours and you're fit enough to climb down 122 steps and then up again.

Oh, and we got the gig at the club. Harry Parfitt changed its name to The Blue Devil and that proved to be an extremely popular decision. We support the main show and the one afterhours, and from time to time we're part of the headliner's line-up.

Come and see us if you're ever in Soho. Smooth and accessible jazz. I know you'll like it.

ABOUT BLUE DEVIL BLUES...

In 2020, I was approached by my writer colleague Alice Bienia to contribute an original short story to an anthology called *Last Shot: Four Tales of Murder, Mystery and Suspense.* My contribution was "Blue Devil Blues". The anthology featured Alice, me and two other Canadian authors, Dwayne Clayden and Peter Kingsmill, and was published in June 2021.

Evie's sanctuary at Romilly Square in "Blue Devil Blues" was inspired, in part, by Down Street, a former Underground station on the Piccadilly line. I've long had an obsession with the Underground—and especially disused stations. Down Street first showed up in my 2001 spy novel, *The Cilla Rose Affair.* I called it Romilly Square and moved it over to the Northern Line and situated it, somewhat impossibly, between Leicester Square and Tottenham Court Road.

When I wrote *The Cilla Rose Affair*, I had no idea what the abandoned underground part of the station looked like. The internet was still in its early days, and photos of its preserved wartime accommodations weren't easily available. So I used my imagination and some creative license.

Romilly Square briefly showed up again in another novel, my 2018 accidental time travel / romantic adventure *Marianne's Memory.*

The London Transport Museum's Hidden London program has, for many years, offered guided tours of disused Underground stations—including Down Street. In 2021, I discovered an online treasure trove of photos, descriptions and sound files from that tour—including a very spooky MP3 recorded in one of its abandoned lift shafts as a train approached, sped past, and then disappeared. The roar of the gale of wind the train generated gave me shivers, and stayed with me as I determined that Romilly Square was going to make one further appearance—this time as Evie's place of refuge in what became "Blue Devil Blues".

Like "Salty Dog Blues", "Blue Devil Blues" features my professional musician/amateur sleuth Jason Davey. It tells the tale of how Jason got his permanent gig at the Blue Devil jazz club in London's Soho.

Chronologically, "Blue Devil Blues" takes place in 2017, five years after *Cold Play*, and before *Disturbing the Peace*.

ABOUT THE AUTHOR

Winona Kent was born in London, England. She immigrated to Canada with her parents at age three, and grew up in Regina, Saskatchewan, where she received her BA in English from the University of Regina. After settling in Vancouver, she graduated from UBC with an MFA in Creative Writing. More recently, she received her diploma in Writing for Screen and TV from Vancouver Film School.

Winona has been a temporary secretary, a travel agent, a screenwriter, the Managing Editor of a literary magazine and a Program Assistant at the School of Population and Public Health at UBC. Her writing breakthrough came many years ago when she won First Prize in the *Flare Magazine* Fiction Contest with her short story about an all-night radio newsman, "Tower of Power." More short stories followed, and then novels.

Winona's debut novel *Skywatcher* was a finalist in the Seal Books First Novel Award and was published by Bantam Books in 1989. Since then, she has written nine more books, including her indie-published Jason Davey Mysteries featuring professional musician / amateur sleuth Jason Davey Figgis.

Winona is currently the national Vice-Chair and the regional BC/YT rep for the Crime Writers of Canada, and is also an active member of Sisters in Crime – Canada West. After many decades working in jobs completely unrelated to writing, Winona recently retired, and is now happily embracing life as a full-time author. She lives in New Westminster, BC.

Please visit her website at www.winonakent.com for more information.

ALSO BY WINONA KENT

The Jason Davey Mysteries
Ticket to Ride
Lost Time
Notes on a Missing G-String
Disturbing the Peace

Other Novels
Marianne's Memory
In Loving Memory
Persistence of Memory
Cold Play
The Cilla Rose Affair
Skywatcher

Manufactured by Amazon.ca
Bolton, ON

34592221R00116